Love's Journey®
ON MANITOULIN ISLAND

Moriah's
FORTRESS

Love's Journey®
ᴏɴ MANITOULIN ISLAND

Moriah's
FORTRESS

BY SERENA B. MILLER

LJ EMORY
PUBLISHING

LJ EMORY
PUBLISHING

Published by L. J. Emory Publishing
Love's Journey is a registered trademark of L. J. Emory Publishing.

First L. J. Emory Publishing trade paperback edition September 2017

For information about special discounts for bulk purchases, please contact L. J. Emory Publishing, sales@ljemorypublishing.com

Printed in the United States of America

10 9 8 7 6 5 4 3 2 1

ISBN 978-1-940283-29-6
ISBN 978-1-940283-30-2 (ebook)

To Steven

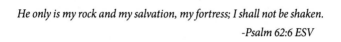

He only is my rock and my salvation, my fortress; I shall not be shaken.

-Psalm 62:6 ESV

Chapter One

May, 1998
Manitoulin Island

Through the dirty window of the old light keeper's office, Moriah watched the wind and rain whip Lake Huron into a frenzy of white topped waves.

The lake had so many moods. There were times when it rested, still and smooth as glass. Other times it was cheerful, lapping at the sandy beach of Tempest Bay as though inviting everyone to come play. In winter it could be treacherous, enticing people out onto ice that was not always as sturdy as it appeared. And some winters it chose to become almost magical by creating glistening ice caves out of the freezing wave action it threw against the shore.

This afternoon, it seemed to be lashing out in hurt and confusion, which perfectly matched her own inner struggle.

"I need to get out of here," she told Ben. "I need to talk to Katherine."

"We'll go soon," Ben said. "It would be suicide to try crossing right now in that metal fishing boat of yours."

"I know." She sighed in frustration.

It was unusual for her to want to leave the ruins of the old lighthouse. For as long as she could remember, it had been her private sanctuary—a fortress against all the things that could go wrong in life.

The day her grandfather died, it was here that she fled, curling up on an old sleeping bag and crying herself sick, while the walls of the light house cradled her. It was within these walls to which she often ran in the summer when the guests at the fishing resort where she worked got on her last nerve. It was here that she had come to recuperate from all the angst and worries she'd experienced during high school.

But the storm combined with the violent nightmare she'd just experienced, made the place feel ominous and threatening today instead of a fortress against life's problems.

She had no idea why her mind had decided to serve up such a nightmare. Ben and she had simply been discussing and making notes on the upcoming restoration of the ruined lighthouse—a pleasant task—when the storm came up and they took shelter inside the keeper's cottage. To while away the time, she'd asked him to tell her about his translation work with the Yahnowa tribe. Unfortunately, she had been exhausted, and had fallen into a half-sleep while he was still talking.

His descriptions of the Yahnowa people and the jungle had somehow brought on such a terrifying nightmare that she was still trembling from the shock of it. In it, she had been a small child in the Yahnowa village, peering through the slats of a neighboring hut while her mother and father were slashed to death by murderous, painted, half-naked Yahnowa men. She'd even dreamed that a man by the name of Petras had stood outside the hut fighting for her life. Petras was Ben's father's name—a fact she didn't remember having ever known.

The whole thing was such a disturbing image it had shaken her to the core, but she knew it could not be based on any sort of real-life experience. Her mother and father had died in a plane crash on their way to do mission work. She had been raised by her grandfather and aunt from the age of five. Except for being orphaned at such an early age, she had lived a very ordinary life.

Her hope was that her aunt might be able to help her figure out why she'd experienced such a mixed up, crazy nightmare. Katherine often knew things that she did not.

***

Ben was nearly as confused as Moriah. Nicolas had never mentioned the fact that Moriah might be the daughter of the missionaries who had been killed in the same massacre that had taken his father. The name of Robertson was a fairly common one. It had never occurred to him that Moriah's parents could have been those people. Especially since Katherine had told him that Moriah's parents had been killed in a plane crash.

And yet...the Yahnowa people still spoke fondly of a little girl who had once lived among them, a child they called Little Green eyes.

Moriah's eyes were strikingly green.

With her screams from the nightmare still ringing in his ears, he decided to not upset her further by mentioning his suspicion to her. If there was any possible way that she *was* the child who had survived the massacre, it was not his place to tell her.

A lightning bolt hit nearby so close that they both jumped. Even though the structure they were in was made of stone, Ben knew they were not safe. His greatest concern was the roof. He hoped it held, but he'd noticed that it was starting to rot in many places. He did not like their chances if the heavy, soggy, roof fell on them.

"It might be best for us to get away from the window," he said. "And it probably wouldn't be a bad idea to stay out of the middle of the room. I know this roof is weak."

Moriah glanced up. "You're right."

She went back to the spot where they had been sitting and dropped down onto the floor. She leaned her back against the stone wall and drew her knees up to her chest, still trembling slightly.

"Are you okay?" Ben sat down beside her.

"I will be," she said. "But I'm having trouble wrapping my mind around what just happened. That nightmare was so real! I can still smell the smoke of the little cooking fire inside the hut."

"Must have been scary."

"It was."

They sat in silence for a while. Then Moriah asked the question he had hoped she wouldn't until he'd had a chance to speak privately with Katherine.

"How did your father die, Ben?"

There it was.

Ben was an awful liar, so as usual, he simply fell back on the truth.

"My father was killed by the Yahnowa, as was Nicolas's mother."

He winced when he heard her sudden intake of breath.

"I'm feeling very confused right now," Moriah said.

"I was just a kid when Dad went there," Ben explained. "My dad met Nicolas's mother, Dr. Janet Bennett, on a trip. He was so impressed and intrigued by her and her work he went to go help in whatever way he could. I stayed with my uncle while he was gone."

"So, you and Nicolas both had parents who were killed by the Yahnowa? When did you find out about each other?"

"We knew of each other from the beginning of my dad and his mother's relationship, but I never met him until last fall. That's when he closed his medical practice and came to see if any of the clinic his mother built in the Amazon still existed."

"Does it?"

"No. At least not much of it. The clinic was abandoned for a long time after Dr. Janet died. Finally, some veteran missionaries, Abraham and Violet Smith, braved going in. The jungle had completely taken over the few structures when I got there. It never was all that much of a place to begin with."

"What about the tribal people?" Moriah asked. "Have they ever talked with you about what happened that night?"

"Not much, and there's no good reason to bring it up. We know what happened. The older ones who still live in the village are embarrassed by what happened. They weren't part of the killings, anyway."

Moriah began to braid a strand of her hair. He'd noticed this before. It seemed to be a reflex comforting action—something to keep her hands busy when she was under stress or thinking hard.

"Do you suppose that was the village where my parents were headed when their plane crashed?" Moriah said. "My grandfather and Katherine never talked much about where my parents were going. I got the feeling it made them sad to talk about it, so I seldom brought it up, but I probably overheard some things over the years. Do you suppose when you started talking about the Yahnowa my brain did something weird with the information and triggered a nightmare?"

Ben dodged the question. "I'm no expert on nightmares."

He noticed a lessening of the wind and rain as the lightning moved further away. Moriah heard it, too.

"The storm is starting to calm down," Moriah said. "Maybe we can leave soon."

"Maybe."

He watched as she rubbed a hand over the cracked linoleum floor. There had once been a floral pattern to it, but most of it had worn off.

"My great-great-grandmother, Eliza Robertson, nearly starved here her first winter. I often wonder what it might have been like to live here back then. "

Ben was grateful for the change of subject. "How much do you know about her?"

"Not a lot. There aren't any written records I've been able to find.

Even the old log book was taken away by the government when the lighthouse was decommissioned. I know her husband, Liam, disappeared and was never found. The spring thaw was late. The lighthouse tender— that's what they call a ship that is specially made to bring supplies to the lighthouses—wasn't able to get through. She had one child with her when it happened, a little boy."

"Did they ever find her husband?"

"No. Once the ship was finally able to break through the ice and get to them, the authorities came and searched. They never found a trace.

A rogue gust of wind blew down the chimney and scattered smoke and embers from the fireplace.

"As first dates go," Ben rubbed the smoke out of his eyes, "I'd say this one has not gone particularly well."

"I was not aware this was a date."

Ben ignored her comment. "Let's see; we've had tears, screams, and nightmares from when you fell asleep. I got scratched up from all the brambles and pine trees I encountered trying to walk that old road here. We're damp from the rain. My backside is killing me from sitting on the floor. I'm hungry. We both smell like smoke. That rain-soaked roof might collapse at any moment. Did I happen to mention I made the acquaintance of a black bear on the way here?"

"You did?" Moriah said.

"I only caught a glimpse of him or her from a distance, but I was impressed." He stretched out his legs. "You sure know how to show a guy a good time, Moriah."

She leaned her head back against the wall beside him. "And to think, I wasn't even trying."

Chapter Two

The rain finally stopped completely. Ben stepped outside for a moment and was treated to the glorious sight of the sun breaking through the clouds over the water.

"It's over," Ben said. "I think we can make it home now."

"Good," she said.

The rainfall had been heavy. When they reached the beached boat, they had to bail out the water before they could climb in. To his surprise, Moriah didn't take over control of the motor. Instead, she chose to sit at the front of the boat.

"You trust me to drive?" he asked, surprised.

"The way I'm feeling right now," she said. "I trust you a whole lot more than I trust myself."

A few minutes later, Ben guided the little fishing boat through waves still choppy from the storm. It felt good to get away from the dark and damp lighthouse. It was one thing to be there when the sun was shining and things were cheerful. It was another thing entirely when it was raining and dreary. Especially when his companion was screaming in terror.

Like Moriah, he couldn't help but wonder how depressing and lonely it must have been for the light keepers and their families when it grew dark out there on the tip of the peninsula, especially when provisions were low and the nearest neighbor was miles away. Those old lighthouse keepers did not have an easy life, no matter how much people tended to romanticize the profession.

Spray from the waves flew into his face. He kept his chin down, trying to avoid as much of it as he could. Moriah faced the front of the boat with face uplifted, as though the spray felt good on her skin. Perhaps, she hoped it would wash away the lingering horror of that terrible dream.

For Moriah's sake, he was trying to act calm about the whole thing, but he had been stunned listening to her describe not only what could have been her mother and father's murder, but his own father's death, as well. He had never known the details of that night. There had been no non-Yahnowa witnesses, except the one child. Now, he would forever bear the image of his father fighting to protect that little girl. It was so typical of his dad.

He could see his father so clearly in his mind. The man had been heavily muscled, even in middle-age. He could just imagine him fighting with those strong, stonemason fists. It was exactly the kind of thing his dad would do. Petras had once been nearly as good of a fighter as he had been a stonemason.

Petras. It meant rock. The name so aptly described the man.

When they reached the small dock, he climbed out and tied off the rope while Moriah stayed huddled in the boat so deep in thought that she didn't seem to notice where she was.

"We're back," he said. "We will soon be warm and dry up at the lodge."

Moriah was young, strong, and healthy. Normally, she bounded out of the boat like it was nothing. Now, she climbed out as stiffly as an old woman. He grabbed her hand and helped steady her.

"A hot bath. Some cocoa. Warm, dry clothes." He steered her toward the lodge. "You'll be as good as new, lass."

He hoped he was right about that. He had never been a lover of secrets, and he had a suspicion there had been way too many of them in the Robertson family.

Chapter Three

"Was it worth it, Kathy?" Nicolas said. "I've always wanted to know."

Katherine's way of dealing with worry and stress was to cook. It had been her release and comfort most of her life. Moriah sometimes joked the amount of food on the table was a good barometer of Katherine's worry level.

At the moment, there was a large pot of chili simmering on the stove, hot cornbread sitting on the counter, a fruit salad in the fridge, and several dozen oatmeal cookies cooling on a white dishcloth spread on the table.

But Katherine was not hungry.

She had been fighting the urge to cook obsessively ever since Nicolas purchased the abandoned lighthouse and moved into one of the vacant cabins at the fishing resort she and Moriah owned.

Actually, she felt a little sick to her stomach, truth be told. Probably because ever since Nicolas had settled into that vacant cabin, he seemed determined to force a conversation between them.

A conversation she absolutely did not want to have.

It had taken a long time for a scab to form over the wound in her heart. It had taken an even longer time for the wound to heal enough that she didn't think about Nicolas every moment of every day. She was terrified if she spent any more time with him the old wound would begin to bleed again. If that happened, she didn't know if it would ever stop.

When would Moriah and Ben get back, anyway? She did not want to be alone with this man.

"Please answer me, Kathy," Nicolas said. "Was it worth it?"

Maybe she should bake a cake. She had all the ingredients. She pulled flour out of the cabinet, found the baking powder...

"Kathy, stop that," Nicolas demanded. "Look at me."

She didn't want to look at him. He looked too good. His dress shirt was opened at the collar and was slightly rumpled. The sleeves were rolled up. His black pants fit him as though they were tailor-made for his body, and knowing Nicolas, they probably were. A lock of dark hair fell over one eye. It gave him a boyish look.

The love of her life, twenty years older, fit and strong and still able to make her heart skip a beat.

She knew she had not aged well. With him gone from her life, there had been no reason to care or fuss about her looks. She didn't so much as own a tube of lipstick anymore. The leather skirt and calico blouse she was wearing was probably the nicest outfit she owned, and it was ancient. She hadn't been to a beauty shop for years.

She had heard his wife was gorgeous and seriously rich.

Would he never leave this lodge?

Suddenly, she heard the sound of a boat motor roaring across the lake.

"Maybe that's Moriah." She headed toward the great room.

From the window, she could see that it was, indeed, Moriah, and Ben was with her. That was even better. She would feed them all and the conversation would be general. And *then* Nicolas would leave. Or she would leave. There was no way she could have the talk he seemed determined to force on her without breaking down. She was on the verge of tears now. And there was no way she was going to cry in front of the man who had abandoned her when she had needed him most.

"You can't avoid me indefinitely, Kathy," Nicolas said. "I'm going to be here all summer. We *are* going to talk."

"Talking won't fix anything, Nicolas."

With an effort, she broke her attention away long enough to greet Moriah and Ben as they came through the door.

"Where have you been?" Katherine asked, her voice more stressed than she intended. "I've been worried."

"We got trapped by the storm out at the lighthouse," Ben said.

"You both look upset." Moriah glanced at Katherine and then at Nicolas. "What's going on?"

Nicolas was silent. He laid his forearm across the thick, wooden mantel and gazed down at the dying fire.

"We were just having a discussion," Katherine said. "It was nothing important."

Nicolas barked out a short laugh as though disagreeing with Katherine's description of the situation.

"There is something weird between you two. There has been from the moment Nicolas arrived. I want to know what it is."

"Leave it alone, Moriah," Katherine said. "Please. It's none of your business."

"I disagree, Kathy." Nicolas turned away from the mantel. "It's very much her business. I think she should know."

"Know what?" Moriah said.

"It's time to tell her," Nicolas said. "She should know what you sacrificed. If you don't, I will. She's not a child anymore."

There was a knock on the door. Ben went to open it.

A family of four were standing outside—a mom, dad, pre-teen son and daughter. All were dressed in white Bermuda shorts, flowered shirts, and flip flops. All were wearing sunglasses. All looked as though they had been taken by surprise with the chilly weather.

"We're the Wrights from Florida," the man said. "We have a reservation."

"Please," Katherine said, grateful for the interruption. "Come inside."

She went to the desk where she took care of the paperwork with the man, while the wife and two teenagers huddled around the fireplace. Nicolas drew away from them and began examining the bookcase although Katherine knew he wasn't particularly interested in any of the dog-eared paperbacks guests had left behind over the years.

The Wrights were interesting. What had they have been thinking when they dressed for this trip? How could they have missed the fact Canada was much further north and colder than Florida?

"How was your trip?" she asked, pleasantly, while Moriah grabbed fresh towels, sheets, and pillowcases and hurriedly ducked out the door to prepare their cabin. Nothing got in the way of taking care of guests. Sickness, worries, emotional storms—the business had to go on.

"Much longer than we expected," Mr. Wright said. "The ferry wasn't running, so we had to go the long way around, up through Michigan."

"I'm sorry to hear that," she said. "But I'm happy you made it here safe and sound."

Her tone was cheerful while she evaluated these new guests. They hadn't realized the ferry wouldn't be running yet? They had not had enough sense to try to make a reservation for the Chi-cheemaun? These people were definitely novices.

She saw Ben throw a couple more logs on the fire to help the Wright family warm up.

"Thanks, Ben."

"No problem," he said. "While you sort everything out here, I'm going to my cabin to change into some dry clothes. I'll be back in a few minutes."

"The weather is a little chilly here at night," Katherine told the family.

"There are usually some sweatshirts and sweaters in the lost-and-found box in the corner. You are welcome to help yourself."

Almost before the words were out of her mouth, the mother was rummaging through the box, tossing sweaters and woolen scarfs to her children. By the time the mother was finished, the whole family looked a little strange in an odd assortment of clothing, but they had stopped shivering.

"I'll show you to your cabin, now," Katherine said.

She was grateful for an excuse to leave the lodge. It would prevent her from spending another minute alone with the man who had broken her heart.

Chapter Four

Moriah had changed into dry clothes and was sitting on the end of one of the couches. A bowl of chili sat untouched beside her on the side table. "The Wrights are set for the night," she said. "We are not expecting any other guests until tomorrow. Now, would you mind telling me what's going on between you two?"

Ben had already consumed two bowls of chili and was giving serious consideration to having a third. He nursed a cup of coffee while he listened.

"Honestly," Katherine said. "It's really not important. Would anyone like more chili?"

"Kathy and I grew up together," Nicolas interrupted with a quick glance at Katherine. "My father left my mother when I was only three. She fought her way through medical school with no help except from your family. My mother and your grandmother were close friends. Both had grown up here on the island."

"Why didn't you tell me about him, Katherine?" Moriah asked. "All these years and you never mentioned knowing Nicolas? Why?"

"Probably because the subject was too painful," Nicolas said. "Am I right, Kathy?"

Katherine bit her lip and nodded.

"My mother dreamed of becoming a medical missionary," Nicolas continued. "I was six when she left me permanently with her friends, the

Robertsons, while she went to establish a medical clinic in the jungles of Brazil."

"She did visit, though," Katherine said.

"Yes, but even when she came here, she went to the reservation every day to help out."

"True," Katherine said. "Nicolas and I would follow her around. She really was quite gifted."

"Brilliant woman, my mom." Nicolas's voice held a tinge of bitterness. "Great doctor. Absentee mother."

Katherine looked around, brightly. "Does anyone want cocoa? Or cookies? I baked cookies."

Ben thought he did...

"Please, Katherine," Moriah said, "I don't want cocoa or cookies. I just want answers."

...and decided he didn't.

Katherine sighed. "I wanted to be a doctor, too, just like her. She always made it seem so noble. I studied hard. I applied for scholarships. Your dad, my big brother, helped. Nicolas and I were in our first year of medical school when we called off our engagement."

"Engagement?" Moriah gaped at them, and Ben choked on his coffee. "You and Nicolas? You have to be kidding! You actually considered marrying someone like Nicolas?"

"He's sitting right here, lass," Ben reminded her. "He can hear you."

"I'm sorry, Nicolas," Moriah said. "But seriously, you and Katherine? It's pretty hard to imagine. She's so kind and caring, and you..."

"And I bought the lighthouse out from under you," Nicolas added. "I committed the unpardonable sin. You've made that abundantly clear."

"Nicolas can come off as being a little cold, sometimes," Katherine said, defensively, "but that isn't who he is. I always knew him as the sweet, shy little boy who cried at night for his mama."

Nicolas made a surprised sound. "You knew about that?"

"I heard you crying, Nicolas," she said. "We all did, but there was nothing any of us could do."

"So why did you break off your engagement?" Moriah began to braid a small lock of her hair nervously.

A long look passed between Katherine and Nicolas. It was a look that went deep. Ben felt like he had just seen a lifetime pass between them.

"Oh, nothing, really," Katherine passed it off. "The timing just wasn't quite right."

"That's the understatement of the century," Nicolas said. "Tell her the truth, Kathy."

"What good will it do?"

Ben felt his stomach tighten, as though anticipating a punch to the gut. Whatever Katherine's next words were, he was fairly certain they were going to hurt Moriah, and from what little he knew, she had been hurt enough.

"Did I have something to do with it?" Moriah said. "Was I the reason you broke off your engagement?"

"After your parents died, the only family you had left was your grandfather and me. Dad was too old to raise you by himself, and he had lost a son, a daughter-in-law, and a beloved wife in the space of two years. I needed to stay and take care of you. I couldn't leave."

A sick dread built inside of Ben as he watched and listened. This story was not going to turn out well.

"Nicolas didn't understand how I could drop out of medical school to care for you. I was a good student, and I worked hard, but he was scary smart. By the time your parents died, he had focused his sights on becoming a top surgeon. He wanted it more than anything else in the world, and he was capable of achieving it."

Katherine looked down at her hands, which were clutched together in her lap.

"So?" Moriah prompted.

"In the end," Katherine's voice was low, "he wanted it more than he wanted me."

Nicolas gazed at Katherine but said nothing. Instead, he slowly shook his head as though refuting everything she had just said.

"Nicolas is a surgeon?" Moriah asked.

"No," Nicolas said, "I'm not a surgeon. My mother was an obstetrician. After her death, I specialized in high risk pregnancies. I suppose I thought it would bring me closer to her, somehow."

"That's why you were able to save Camellia's baby."

"Camellia's birth was easy, compared to some of the situations I've had to deal with, but yes, that's why I was able to help her."

"So, let me see if I understand what you're saying," Moriah said. "You, Katherine, thought you could not leave the island because of me. You quit medical school because I went into a meltdown every time you tried to take me across the bridge, and you didn't feel like you could dump me on my grandfather. And Nicolas, you couldn't face being tied down forever on Manitoulin Island. Is that correct? Am I reading this right? I managed to ruin both of your lives?"

"You couldn't help any of it," Katherine said. "You were a child. I was only twenty-two, myself. Too young to know how to help you. Not wise enough to deal with your problems in a healthy way. All I knew to do was to keep reassuring you that you were safe here with me, but my reassurances apparently only made the situation worse. Besides, if Nicolas had loved me enough, he would have found a way to work something out. He married within the year." Katherine glanced at Nicolas as she continued. "I heard his wife was very beautiful and quite wealthy."

"Correction," Nicolas said. "If you had loved *me* enough, *you* would have found a way. And for the record, I soon discovered that my 'beautiful' wife was incapable of loving anyone besides herself. I made a terrible mistake, but I was already bound to her by the time I found out."

"Then why did you stay with her?"

"I am not my father. I had made a vow to her, and I kept it."

Nicolas and Katherine were so intent on one another they had apparently forgotten Ben and Moriah were in the room.

"You were the one I loved, Kathy. Always. From the time we were children. You were the only one. My marriage was created in a selfish fit of temper and I have suffered a lifetime for it."

"You did throw a lot of tantrums when we were small," Katherine smiled, remembering. "They were memorable, but they never accomplished much."

"I grew up, Kathy. My wife died fourteen months ago. I cared for her until the end." He waited for the impact of these words to sink in. "I've done a lot of good with my life. I've done the best I knew how. But now, all I really want to do is come home. That's the only reason I bought the lighthouse, Kathy. I'm so tired. I just want to come home."

Katherine, who was seated in one of the leather chairs, hesitated a moment, then she reached out her arms to him. Nicolas rushed over, knelt in front of her and they embraced. Nicolas held onto to Katherine like a drowning man, as she stroked his hair and crooned soothing words.

"This is our cue to leave," Ben whispered to Moriah.

"I know," Moriah said, "but I still need to ask Katherine about my nightmare."

"Later," Ben said. "Those two deserve some time alone."

"I'll see you in the morning, then." Moriah reluctantly went upstairs, and Ben let himself out while Nicolas and Katherine simply clung to one another.

Chapter Five

Ben, a good night's sleep under his belt, filled with hot oatmeal and good-will toward men, walked toward the lodge in the early morning sunshine. He could hardly wait to see what new things might transpire today. Being around Katherine, Moriah, and Nicolas was nearly as good as having television, except it was real people dealing with real problems. He genuinely wanted only the best for all of them.

When he arrived at the lodge, Katherine was bustling around the kitchen and she was humming. That was new. She was dressed in her buckskin outfit again, so he supposed she was going to work today. Nicolas was standing over a skillet of scrambled eggs with a spatula in his hand. He was wearing khaki pants with a plaid shirt. His shirt was not tucked in. For Nicolas, this was casual in the extreme.

Moriah came in about the same time as Ben. She was ready for work, dressed in a brown flannel shirt and jeans, her hair pulled back into a tight braid. He searched her face. She didn't look like she had slept well.

"There's fresh juice in the fridge if you want some," Katherine said. "We'll have breakfast ready in a jiffy. Are you eating with us, Ben?"

Ben could smell bacon in the oven. Suddenly, hot oatmeal didn't seem like nearly enough breakfast to get him through the morning.

"Sure!"

"By the way," Katherine said, "I called Sam Black Hawk early yesterday morning. He specializes in snakes. Sam promised to come take a look at our little problem under Cabin One."

"Does he think he can help?" Moriah asked.

"He said not to worry; he can take care of it."

"Great. I was beginning to think I'd have to burn down the cabin and start all over."

"I don't think he has anything that drastic planned."

"Will it be expensive?"

"Probably not. Your grandfather was a good friend to Sam, and I helped his mother get through some difficult times. He seemed happy for a chance to help us."

"That's a relief."

The radio was playing soft, classical music as Katherine pulled the pan of crisp bacon from the oven and plated it. Nicolas dished out the eggs; Ben made himself useful by pouring out the juice. Moriah buttered the toast, then brought out the plates and silverware. Katherine made fresh coffee. The morning sun poured through the windows.

Everything was lovely as Katherine asked Ben to say grace. He did, with thankfulness pouring from his heart. As they ate, he felt blessed to be sitting with these people in this room at this moment. Life was good until Moriah spoke.

"Why did you lie to me, Katherine?"

Ben sighed inwardly. Things had been going so well.

"My love for Nicolas was a painful memory." Katherine said. "I had no desire to relive it by sharing it."

"I'm not talking about Nicolas."

Katherine looked puzzled.

Moriah carefully laid her knife and fork on her plate. "Tell me about my mom and dad's death."

Katherine hesitated. "Your parents died in a plane crash on their way to do mission work. You know that."

"Why was I not with them?" Moriah asked. "You told me last night that you were in medical school. My grandmother was already gone. Even though my grandfather was always kind to me, I doubt my parents would have left a five-year-old alone with him for an extended period of time. Why was I not in the plane with them?"

Ben watched Katherine struggle for an answer. Moriah's logic had blindsided her. She had no ready explanation.

"You were the one person in the world I trusted completely," Moriah said, when Katherine didn't answer. "Why did you feel the need to lie to me about how my parents died?"

"She was afraid you would stop talking again." Nicolas intervened. "She couldn't bear to see you re-traumatized and was afraid that's what would happen if you knew."

"If I knew what?" Moriah crossed her arms. "What exactly were you afraid that I would find out?"

"She's a grown woman now, Kathy," Nicolas said. "She deserves to know the truth."

"I was there, wasn't I?" Moriah said. "I actually saw my parents being murdered."

It took a moment for Katherine to answer, but when she did, her voice was low and steady. "You were a child. I did what I thought was best for you."

"I've been an adult for a long time."

"You seemed to remember nothing," Katherine said. "Considering the horror of what you had been through, I thought that was a good thing. I was grateful. The last thing I wanted was to bring any of it back to mind. Even your doctor thought it best not to bring it all back up. I believe his words were something along the lines of letting sleeping dogs lie."

"I think those sleeping dogs have awakened," Ben said. "Tell them

31

what happened yesterday at the lighthouse, Moriah."

She described the nightmare in all its horrific detail.

When she was finished, no one said anything or wanted breakfast anymore, not even Ben. When no one made any comment, Moriah got up and walked out of the room. Nicolas quietly cleared the table. Ben went to the porch and watched Moriah walk away along the water's edge. It did not seem wise to him to follow her, but he could keep an eye on her from this vantage point. Katherine came to stand beside him, also watching. Every now and then, they would see her stop, stare at the lake and then start walking again.

"The bodies were too mutilated and decayed to bring home," Katherine said. "Who tells a child something like that? I certainly couldn't. I bought a headstone to put in the church cemetery with the names of Jacob and Mary Ann Robertson on it. I wanted to create a place where Moriah could lay flowers on her parent's grave, but nothing is there except the headstone. I did what I thought was best. Maybe I was wrong."

Katherine shook her head with regret, then walked back inside the lodge.

For the first time since arriving on the island, Ben almost wished he was back with the Yahnowa. He hated to see such suffering. Especially when there was nothing he could do about it.

After a while, he saw Moriah turn back toward the lodge. Her steps were steady. There was a determination to her pace. Apparently, she had come to some sort of a conclusion during her solitary walk.

He went inside the lodge where Nicolas and Katherine were washing dishes. "She's coming back."

"Thanks for warning us," Nicolas said.

The three of them were seated in the great room when she entered. All three were steeled to answer whatever she asked. They heard her mount the wooden porch steps. Then the door swung open. She stood there with her feet braced. Hands clenched. Cheeks flushed. Her hair had come loose from its braid. She had obviously prepared herself to face whatever they told her.

"So, what happened?" she said. "I'm not five anymore and I need to know."

Chapter Six

The more they talked, the more Moriah realized somewhere in the back of her mind, much of this information had been stored. Apparently, her mind had been either unwilling or unable to examine it until now.

"My mother," Nicolas explained, "managed accidentally to do something that set one of the tribal headmen off. I've not been able to find out what it was, nor has Ben. We're still not sure exactly what happened. Most of the Yahnowa were grateful she was there. But one particular man, Chief Moawa, who was from a neighboring Yahnowa tribe, was not happy with her. He gathered several of the younger men and got them stirred up about the outsiders. Unfortunately, in addition to my mother, the 'outsiders' happened to be Ben's father and your parents. They were innocents, just trying to help make a better life for these people."

"And I was there."

"You were there," Katherine said. "Apparently, you saw it all. The only thing that saved your life was you were spending the night with a little friend in the hut across from the clinic. That family hid you and got you out of the village before Chief Moawa figured out where you were. They put themselves in great danger to do so. What little we know about what happened, we found out from the Catholic priest to whom the family took you. They didn't know what else to do. He brought you to Detroit and that's where Dad and I got you. I've never been so happy to see someone in my life."

"So, you remember everything now?" Nicolas said.

"I don't know. I think I witnessed my father and Petras trying to protect Dr. Janet and Mom. And at the very end, I'm fairly certain Petras was fighting to protect me."

"Please don't be angry at me," Katherine said. "Your doctor said it would be best if the memories came back on their own. He said if we told you about it before you were ready, it might reopen wounds you couldn't deal with. You were so little and you were so traumatized."

"But why did you make up the story about the plane crash?"

"Once you began to speak again, you started asking where your parents were. I had to tell you something, but how could I tell a fragile five year old her parents had been murdered? Maybe it was wrong. I don't know. I'm sorry you're hurt. But I was trying to do the best I could for you."

"You've had a lot of years to tell me the truth."

"When would you have been ready to hear your parents had been hacked to death by the very tribe they were trying to help? Did I really need to put that image in your mind?" Katherine pressed her hand against her heart. "I didn't even want that image to remain within my *own* memory! I didn't know what to do, nor did your grandfather. We decided to try to give you the most normal childhood we could. I'm sorry if that wasn't enough."

"I don't know if you did the right thing, either, Katherine. I really don't, but I understand why you did it," Moriah said. "I also appreciate how good you have been to me, and the sacrifices you've made down through the years. What I don't understand is why you, Ben, chose to work and live where your father was killed. How could you do that?"

"I have a gift for languages, Moriah. They come easily for me. When I started considering where I might best use my gift, the first place that came to mind was the Yahnowa tribe. It was a way to continue my dad's work. I didn't want his death to be in vain."

"And Nicolas, you have recently gone back there also. Why?"

"The main culprit," Nicolas explained, "was Chief Moawa. He gave the young men who followed him jungle intoxicants. Afterward, there was no more clinic, and they were sorry. But by then, it was too late. I tried to ignore that place for a long time, but in the end, I had to go back. When I saw what Ben was doing, I decided to help. Once we get the lighthouse finished, I'll concentrate on seeing what I can do to fulfill my mother's dream."

"I see." Moriah voice was bone tired.

"I know all this is a shock," Katherine said. "Would you like to go lie down for a bit?"

"I would very much like to crawl into bed, pull the covers over my head, and stay there until my life makes sense again. But…" She glanced at the wall clock and stood up wearily. "Dale Trowbridge will be here any minute with that big load of gravel I ordered for the driveway. I need to get things ready to start spreading it."

"I can take care of that," Ben said. "Nicolas can help me."

Nicolas seemed a little surprised to be included in a project that required manual labor, but he agreed as well. "Yes, I'll help, too."

Ben was happy he'd offered when he saw the look of relief on Moriah's face. That job would take her, working alone, the rest of the day or longer. Helping was the least they could do.

"Thanks," she said. "I appreciate it. The rakes and shovels are in the tool shed. Nicolas, grab some work gloves or you'll get blisters. Katherine, you'll need to write a check when Dale gets here."

The gravel came, the check was written, and Ben and Nicolas spent several hours helping rake two truckloads of gravel smoothly over the driveway. The sun was setting when they finished. Moriah took off her hat, leaned on her rake, and surveyed the work they had done.

"It looks good. Having you two help made a huge difference."

"*Now* you can go to bed and pull the covers over your head," Ben said. He wasn't joking. Moriah was so tired she appeared to be standing only by sheer will-power. There were dark circles beneath her eyes that had not been there the day he met her. Struggling with the realities of her past was taking a toll.

"I believe I will do just that." She walked away, carrying her rake with her.

"By the way." She stopped and turned to face them. "If you two still want me to help pull the lighthouse project together, I'll do it."

"Great! What changed your mind?" Ben asked.

"If both of you can be forgiving enough to go back to the people who killed your parents, I guess I should do the same."

"You are thinking of going to the Amazon?" Nicolas asked.

"Of course not," Moriah said. "Didn't you say that you will start concentrating on fulfilling your mother's dream after we get the lighthouse project finished?"

"I did."

"I can help you get it done faster. Ben's right. I do know all the contractors and skilled labor on the island. I know who we can trust to show up for work and do a good job. I can save you a lot of headaches."

"That's a relief," Nicolas said. "Thank you!"

"You're welcome. Frankly, I think both of you need to have your heads examined going back there. I never want to see that place again as long as I live. But I can help move your schedule up. Consider it my contribution."

Moriah hefted her rake and left without another word.

"She's probably right." Ben smiled. "We probably do need to have our heads examined."

"All I can think about is Katherine, right now, anyway." Nicolas shrugged. "Wouldn't it be something if we got back together after all these years?"

"It would," Ben said. "I think I'm going to head back to my cabin now. I have no plans to go to bed and pull the covers over my head, but I do have some work to do."

He saw that he was talking to Nicolas's back. The man had already headed back to the lodge. He thought Nicolas acted as though he was afraid Katherine would disappear if he didn't keep her in eyesight at all times.

When Ben got back to his cabin, he pulled his sketch pad out of his backpack and looked long and hard at the rough drawing he'd made of Moriah while she had been asleep out at the lighthouse. That was before the nightmare, when things were still relatively simple. The drawing had turned out pretty well. He tore it off the tablet and stuck it into the corner of the frame of an old picture. It gave him pleasure to see it there.

Then he sat down at his desk and began to sketch again. This time, it was the light tower and cottage. He was getting a good understanding of how to recreate both into something everyone could be proud of when the job was finished.

Now that all the secrets had been brought out into the open and forgiven, he thought life was going to be much easier for everyone.

***

Moriah showered off the gravel dust and sweat from leveling the driveway, wrapped her hair in a towel, donned her robe, and went to her bedroom. There, she softly closed the door and locked it. There was no need for a lock, and she seldom used it. Katherine would never walk in without knocking. They always respected one another's privacy. Nor was she concerned about guests wandering in. The great room downstairs in the lodge where they greeted and checked in guests was, by necessity, a public place, but a sign at the bottom of the steps let everyone know the upstairs was private living quarters. So far, no one had ever been rude enough to ignore the fact.

There was no reason at all for her to lock her door tonight, except it made her feel a little better. She needed to shut out the world tonight. The day had been overwhelming in every way.

She tossed the damp towel on the foot of her bed, combed out her wet hair, exchanged her robe for flannel pajamas, and then fell face forward on her bed. If any of her guests had an issue in the middle of the night, Katherine would have to take care of it. Moriah was done.

Then she opened one eye and noticed her giant globe sitting in the corner. She crawled off the bed, gave the globe a spin, closed her eyes, and let her finger glide over the surface until the globe stopped spinning. Then she opened her eyes and peeked beneath her finger. Trinidad. That would be a nice place to visit. It would always be warm in Trinidad.

For a moment, she gave into a fantasy of stepping onto an airplane, flying to Trinidad, and exploring the island. What wonders would she discover there if she ever got to go?

Unless something changed drastically within her, that was something she would never know.

Chapter Seven

. . . .

"Why did they let it grow up?" Ben shoved his fingers through his hair as he stared at the wall of new-growth forest and brambles that stood between him and Robertson's lighthouse.

His hair was getting so long it was starting to bother him. Maybe he should talk Moriah into cutting it. Then it hit him that Moriah cutting it would also involve Moriah running her fingers through his hair. The thought made his knees go weak, so maybe that wasn't such a good idea. He needed to find a barber, preferably a male barber.

He reminded himself it would not be wise to get romantically involved with Moriah. As much as he admired her, now that he knew everything, falling in love with her would be a disaster. He had important work to do in Brazil, and she would be a hindrance. The girl needed a nice, normal Manitoulin Islander man in her future, not him.

"It was never more than packed dirt, anyway." Standing a few paces in front of him, Moriah jammed her hands into her back pockets and planted her boots firmly apart as she surveyed the dense woods. A dark blue baseball cap printed with the words "Robertson's Resort" was pulled low. Her plain, white tank top showed off the firm muscle in her upper arms and back.

To Ben, her stance was entrancing. She was especially cute when in full work-mode.

Forget it, McCain, he warned himself again. He forced his attention away from Moriah and back to the subject at hand.

She seemed completely unaware of his attention. "After the Fresnel lens was stolen, the Coast Guard deliberately let the road grow over to discourage sightseers and vandals."

"That's the third time you've mentioned a Fresnel lens. What's so special about it?"

"It was revolutionary. In the early 1800's, when most of the light towers were built, the lights on the Great Lakes were nothing more than oil-burning lamps with reflectors behind them. It required as many as ten lamps to make a light bright enough to warn a ship. Then, a Frenchman by the name of Fresnel experimented with creating layers of specially cut glass surrounding and reflecting one lamp. A Fresnel lens is lovely. It looks sort of like a huge, multifaceted diamond with a light glowing inside. I've seen miniature replicas sold as jewelry in lighthouse catalogs. Ours was called a second order light, which was one of the largest on the lakes. It was nearly as tall as a man."

"And it's not possible to buy one anymore?"

"Not to my knowledge. I don't know where you could ever get one, unless you could talk a museum out of one of them, which is not likely. There are lighthouse history buffs who keep lists of every Fresnel lighthouse lens known. Even the one we had wasn't new when it arrived, back in the 1800's."

"How did your people end up with a used lens?"

"It started out inside a light tower on the shores of southern Georgia. The light keeper grew so afraid the Union army would destroy or take it that he secretly dismantled and buried each lens in the sand. The story goes that he was so destitute after the war, he secretly sold it and blamed it's disappearance on the Union troops."

"When did it disappear from the Robertson lighthouse?"

"Soon after my grandfather's death. The Coast Guard had already installed their automated light pole, but the road was still passable then. The lighthouse became a favorite place for late-night beach parties, and since we didn't own it, there was nothing Katherine nor I could do. The lens disappeared soon after. It was either destroyed, or someone got a lot of money for it. There's an extremely strong market for original lighthouse memorabilia."

"Did you know your grandfather well?"

"He helped Katherine raise me as long as he was able. I learned quite a few things about tools and carpentry trotting around behind him, getting underfoot. Eventually, I became competent enough to be a bit of help to him. I was thirteen when he died."

Moriah pulled off the baseball cap and let her hair swing free, ruffling it with her fingers.

"It's warm this morning." She twisted her hair into a loose knot and tucked it beneath her cap again. It was such an innocent, womanly gesture that it made Ben swallow hard.

Even though he had only known her a few days, he wished with all his heart it was within his power to give her the lighthouse for her own. He also wished he could give her the Fresnel lens and, while he was at it, the sun, the moon, and the stars. But he was just a stonemason, not a magician. The best he could do was put the tower back together. Maybe seeing it in good repair would be gift enough.

He cleared his throat. "Well, we can't start until we get a road in. Are you sure you're okay helping me with this project?"

"I am," she said. "Even if I don't own it, I couldn't bear to see someone else mess it up. There might be some on the island who are better carpenters, but no one cares about it more than me. It would probably drive me nuts not to be involved in bringing it back to life."

Ben felt a combination of relief and excitement tinged with worry. To have Moriah around all summer as they worked on a project together—well, he wasn't sure life could get much better than that. But, he reminded himself yet again, he couldn't afford to get too attached to the girl.

"The road is impassable," he said. "I barely made it through that one time I walked to the lighthouse to see you. We'll have to make it into a road again before we can do anything else. Do you know of a good heavy equipment operator?"

"Let's go see my buddy, Jack." Moriah turned toward him and smiled. "He can use the work, and you'll like him."

"I don't have to like him. All I need to know—is he any good?"

"Jack is so good, he can just about do brain surgery with a backhoe." Moriah tossed him the keys to her truck. "You drive."

Chapter Eight

After driving a couple of miles, Moriah directed him to pull into the driveway of a small, white frame house. Beside it stood two bulldozers, one slightly larger and newer than the other, as well as a backhoe and a large flatbed trailer. In front of the garage was a red Ford pickup.

Her buddy, Jack, might be a great heavy equipment operator, but apparently he didn't know how to operate a lawnmower. Knee high weeds and grass decorated the front yard.

"Your friend's not much into yard maintenance, is he?" Ben followed Moriah up the front steps.

"He's pretty busy," she admitted, "but it isn't usually this bad. Jack's proud of his home. He worked hard to buy it. He and Alicia have probably just been a little overwhelmed with their new baby."

Moriah knocked, but no one answered the door.

"That's odd. His truck's here." She knocked again. "He's usually wherever that truck is."

When no one came to the door, she tried the doorknob. It opened easily. Moriah poked her head in and gasped. Ben looked over her shoulder. The living room had been completely trashed. The couch had been overturned, pictures hung askew on the walls, and curtains puddled on the floor. The place looked like a tornado had hit it, except there had been no tornado.

"Jack?" she called.

No answer.

"Jack? It's Moriah. Are you home?"

"Maybe we should call the police," Ben suggested.

Moriah ignored him. "Jack?" She tiptoed down a hallway, peeking into each room. Ben stopped and stared at the kitchen as he followed her. Every cabinet hung open; every piece of china lay smashed on the floor. Someone with a violent temper had definitely been at work here. Feelings of *deja vu* swept over him. This scene was sickeningly familiar to him.

"Ben!" Moriah called from the back of the house. "Come here. Quick. Something is wrong with Jack!"

Ben made his way toward her voice. He passed a room to the left of the hallway and glanced in. Unlike the rest of the house, peace and order reigned within. It was a nursery, pink, pristine and perfect. At least, in there, nothing had been disturbed.

At the end of the hall, in the master bedroom, stench and filth greeted him.

A man, whom Ben presumed to be the marvelous backhoe operator, Jack, lay clothed in pajama bottoms on a disheveled bed. Dirty clothes and decaying food were scattered about.

Moriah stood in the middle of the disarray, looking bewildered and vulnerable.

"Jack?" She bent over and shook the inert figure on the bed. "Where's Alicia and little Betsy?"

The man mumbled something into the pillow along the lines of wanting to be left alone.

"Please, Jack. Tell me what's wrong." She shook his shoulder again. "Are you sick?"

Ben leaned against the doorframe, crossed his arms, and took in the situation. It wasn't hard to read. What surprised him was that Moriah didn't seem to understand what was going on.

"Does your friend like to drink, by any chance?" Ben asked.

"A little," Moriah said, "but he stopped when he fell in love with Alicia. She wouldn't marry him unless he did."

"I think he might have started again."

"Is that what's wrong with him?" She glanced up at Ben from Jack's bedside. "He's not sick? He's just drunk?"

"Yep. You need to leave, Moriah," he said. "Let me take care of this."

"But, what if he needs…"

"Out!" He wanted Moriah gone from this stinking room. "Now. Please."

With one last glance of concern for Jack, Moriah obeyed.

"Get up," Ben growled at the semi-conscious figure, once he heard Moriah moving around in the kitchen.

"Leave me alone."

"Get *up*!" Ben fisted his hand in Jack's dirty blonde hair. The desire to shake some sense into the man was overwhelming. This was Moriah's good friend?

Jack opened one red-rimmed eye, squinted, and peered at him. "Who are you?"

"I *was* the man who was going to give you a good job for the summer. I don't think that's going to happen now."

Jack let loose a string of curses, then awkwardly swung his legs over the side of the bed and pulled himself up into a sitting position.

"Was that Moriah in here?"

"Yes."

Another string of expletives split the air. "I didn't want her to see me like this." He leaned over and cradled his head in his hands.

"Where are your wife and baby?"

"I didn't touch them if that's what you're thinking."

"Did you do all this damage while they were still here?"

"No. After they left. Quit asking me questions; my head hurts."

Ben breathed a sigh of relief. He hoped Jack was telling the truth.

"How long have they been gone?"

"What day is it?" Jack scrubbed his hands over his face, as though trying to wake himself up.

"Saturday."

"Alicia took Betsy to her mother's two weeks ago."

"Good for her," Ben said.

"I'm not a drunk." Jack glared at Ben.

"Could've fooled me."

"She shouldn't have left." Jack shook his head. "I need her with me to stay sober."

"Your wife showed good sense. She got herself and your baby to a safe place. Now, get up before Moriah comes in to check on you again. I hear her out there, right now, trying to clean up the mess you made."

"I was mad." Jack stumbled to his feet, knocking over the bedside lamp in the process.

"Mad is a choice." Ben righted the lamp and shoved his shoulder under the swaying man. "So is being stupid."

Chapter Nine

Moriah heard the shower turn on. She peeked around the kitchen door as Ben came out of the bathroom and marched down the hallway. He emerged a moment later, grim-faced, steering a wobbly Jack from the bedroom into the bathroom.

She decided to trust Ben with her friend and returned to the task of retrieving broken crockery off the floor and dropping the pieces into a trash can she had found in the adjoining laundry room. Alicia would be so upset if she came home and found her kitchen like this.

A thump and a groan came from the bathroom then a yelp. She didn't know exactly what was going on in there, but she heard steel in Ben's voice as it penetrated into the kitchen.

"I don't *care* if you don't want to take a shower," Ben said. "You stink, man. I'm not letting you near Moriah until you clean up."

She decided she didn't envy Jack one bit. He was the larger man of the two, but Ben was built like a rock. If Jack was putting up a fight about taking a shower, she would bet on Ben winning.

The last shard of pottery had been gathered when the bathroom door banged open and Jack staggered out. He was dressed in clean clothes, and his hair was combed. Ben steadied him from behind.

Ben's longish red hair had curled in the steam of the bathroom, giving him a wild look. His jaw was set. His shirt was drenched. His eyes blazed, but his voice was under control. He spoke to her with a calm that belied those smoldering eyes.

"I think some black coffee might be a good idea, Moriah, if you don't mind."

"All the coffee cups are broken," she said. "Maybe we could go down to the lodge and get some?"

Ben propped Jack against the wall with one hand, reached into his own pocket, and handed her the keys. "Good idea. You drive."

Chapter Ten

The cab of the truck was too small for three grown people to sit comfortably. Moriah's shoulder was wedged tightly against the side of her door as she drove. No one spoke, not even when they arrived at the resort.

Ben pulled Jack out of the truck and guided him up the steps into the lodge, while Moriah followed. Fortunately, Katherine was already in the kitchen preparing lunch. A coffee maker gurgled merrily on the counter. The cozy scene was reassuring to Moriah after the chaos of Jack's house. Nicolas was sitting at the kitchen table working a crossword puzzle. Katherine was humming a little song and smiling as she worked at the counter.

"Jack needs some black coffee, Katherine, if you don't mind." Ben sat the blonde man down at the kitchen table beside Nicolas and pulled out a chair for himself.

Katherine turned away from her lunch preparations and took in the situation.

"The coffee isn't quite finished yet. Have you eaten today, Jack?"

"No, ma'am," Jack mumbled.

"I have chicken salad sandwiches and vegetable soup."

"Thank you, ma'am."

Katherine looked at Ben and Moriah. "What about the two of you?"

"I'm not hungry." After working on Jack's nasty kitchen, Moriah thought it might be a while before she felt hungry again.

"I'd like some, if there's enough," Ben said.

"I made plenty." Katherine turned back to the stove and stirred a pot. "Nicolas and I were making plans while I chopped vegetables, and I'm afraid I accidentally made enough soup to feed a small army."

"Plans?" Moriah reached to take two bright yellow soup bowls out of the cupboard.

"Your aunt and I are getting married!" Nicolas announced.

Moriah froze. "*Excuse* me?"

"It's true." Katherine said. "Please be happy for me."

One of the soup bowls slipped from Moriah's grasp and crashed to the floor. She stared at it, focusing on the yellow pieces. More broken crockery to deal with.

"You're joking." Moriah's voice quavered in spite of her attempt to steady it. "Right?"

"Kathy and I have always loved each other," Nicolas said.

The fact he had announced their plans instead of allowing Katherine to do so, annoyed Moriah almost as much as the announcement itself. Besides, her nerves were already on edge.

"You think the fact you played together as kids gives you the right to come in here and marry my aunt?" Moriah said. "You dumped her. Remember? Just because you didn't want to be burdened with me."

"No, Moriah. We're not joking." Katherine gazed at her steadily, as though waiting for her reaction to run its course. "I've never been surer of anything in my life."

Moriah knew she needed to be careful about what came out of her mouth next. Very deliberately, she sat the remaining bowl on the counter. "When?"

"Soon," Nicolas answered, "sometime this summer, as soon as you and your aunt get through the worst of tourist season and can have some time to prepare for a wedding. You'll be Kathy's maid of honor, of course."

Now, he was telling her who would be Katherine's maid of honor? That was her aunt's place, not his. This man would take over their lives entirely if Katherine married him. In fact, it looked like he already was.

Moriah was so exasperated she spoke without thinking. "Have you lost your mind, Katherine?"

Katherine's expression of happiness melted, and Moriah watched her aunt's face freeze into her professional expression of calm—effectively shutting her out.

"As a matter of fact," Katherine lifted her chin as though daring her niece to argue with her, "I've not lost my mind. I feel like I've finally found it. I've thought of Nicolas every day for years. There's no need for us to lose any more of our lives. We might not even wait until the end of summer. We might just go to the courthouse tomorrow. So, don't worry about being my maid of honor. I'm too old for a formal wedding, anyway."

"But you said…" Nicolas objected.

"That was just daydreaming, Nicolas. A church wedding would look silly for an old maid like me."

"Excuse me," Ben interrupted. "Is that coffee ready, yet?"

Moriah glanced at Jack, who seemed ready to slide beneath the table. She quickly selected the largest mug she could find and filled it to the brim. The coffee hadn't finished flowing through the coffee maker and several dribbles sizzled on the burner. She didn't care. Her hand shook as she poured.

Her aunt, her rock, was getting married to a man who got on Moriah's nerves with every word he spoke. Every time she thought Nicolas was becoming likable—for instance, when he helped her and Ben with the driveway—he'd say something that would set her teeth on edge again. Just thinking about the ramifications of him coming into their lives so intimately made her stomach feel queasy.

Things had been so much simpler before he showed up.

She handed the cup to Ben, willing him to take Jack and leave the kitchen so she could have it out with Katherine and Nicolas. As she bent to give him the cup, he whispered in her ear. "Be careful, Moriah. You've already said too much."

She jerked upright. Be careful indeed. It wasn't *his* aunt getting married to this man. "Can we go someplace a little more private and talk, Katherine?"

"Maybe later, dear. Nicolas and I have more to discuss." Katherine ladled soup into a bowl and placed it in front of Jack. "By the way, now that Nicolas has retired from his obstetrics practice, he says he thinks he would enjoy having a hand in running the resort. You'll be working on the lighthouse anyway, and I could use the help."

Moriah looked at Katherine and saw her aunt's heart in her eyes. *Please,* Katherine's eyes pleaded. *Please don't ruin this for me.*

The room was silent as though everyone, including Jack, were waiting for Moriah to release them from some sort of evil spell. Nicolas didn't even look at her. He just toyed with the edge of his napkin, probably waiting for another outburst.

Twenty years her aunt had pined for him? Twenty years with no other man in her life?

There really was no accounting for taste.

Moriah loved her aunt. She realized there was only one decision she could make if she was to keep their relationship intact.

"Congratulations, Katherine." She put her arms around her aunt. "You deserve all the happiness in the world. I'll be honored to be your maid of honor, and I'm happy Nicolas will be helping you with the resort this summer."

Still hugging her aunt, she narrowed her eyes and gave Nicolas a meaningful look over her aunt's shoulder. She hoped the message was clear to him. Don't even think about hurting this woman again, or you'll have me to deal with.

Chapter Eleven

Ben found Moriah later, on the roof of Cabin Four, pounding nails into shingles with much more force than necessary.

"I drove Jack home," he called up to her.

She sunk a nail.

"We cleaned the rest of the trash out of the house."

She sunk another one.

"Can you hear what I'm saying?"

"Make yourself useful, Ben. Bring me up some more nails."

Ben found a box of unopened nails lying near the house's foundation. He grabbed them and mounted the ladder.

"Did you hear anything I said?" He poked his head over the edge of the roof.

"I heard." She furiously pounded two more nails into the gray shingles then tossed the used-up empty box to the ground and motioned for him to come the rest of the way up.

Ben crept across the roof to sit beside her.

"Nice place." He laid the fresh box of nails on the roof near her feet, hoping she wouldn't accidentally brain him with the hammer. "You come here often?"

Moriah slid him an angry glance, grabbed some nails, held them between her lips, and started nailing again.

Ben wasn't entirely certain he was safe up here with her so angry, so he scooted away and prepared to descend.

"Please don't go," Moriah mumbled around a mouthful of nails.

Ben contemplated the risk, then he scooted close and tried to comfort her by patting her on the back.

"You'll get used to him being around," he said. "Nicolas might even be useful. Maybe you won't have to work so hard if he's helping at the resort."

"Seriously?" Moriah spit the nails into her hand. "Can you picture Nicolas crawling underneath one of the cabins to fix the plumbing? Or unplugging a toilet? Or doing anything useful?"

"He certainly knows how to deliver a baby and rake gravel," Ben said. "You have to give him that. And he makes your aunt happy."

It really wasn't all that bad, he thought, sitting on top of a roof in Canada in the spring sunshine with a beautiful woman. She smelled faintly of sun and strawberry shampoo. Things could be worse. He could be Jack, for instance.

Speaking of which, he had good news that might cheer her up.

"I told Jack he could ride with us to church next week."

She pulled away to stare at him.

"Jack agreed to go to church?"

"Yes."

"I'm surprised. Jack's a great guy, but he hates church."

"Yes, he made that clear, but he's not a great guy, Moriah. He's an angry drunk. How long has he been like this?"

"I don't know. He used to drink when he was younger, but when he fell in love with Alicia, that all changed. I wonder what set him off?"

"Apparently, he hasn't had a lot of work lately. He broke his promise to her, had some beer with some friends. She found out and got upset, and then he got upset; Then she left, and instead of going after her, he made the brilliant decision to binge."

"How on earth did you talk him into going to church?"

"I kind of made it a prerequisite of getting the job. Plus, I told him if he wants to work for us for the summer, I'll need proof he's going to AA every week."

"You blackmailed him into staying sober by offering a job." She laughed. "That's not fair."

"Of course, it isn't. But whatever works." Ben was silent for a moment, thinking and remembering. "Did he ever hit Alicia or the baby?"

"Not to my knowledge. Jack's more likely to take it out on things."

"What do you mean?"

"I saw him put his fist through a windshield once."

"Whose windshield?"

"His own."

"Good for him!" Ben said.

"Seriously?"

"I think Jack might be a lot like my Dad used to be," Ben said, "except Dad sometimes hit people instead of things."

Moriah caught her breath at this revelation. "Your dad hit you?"

"Sometimes." His eyes were on the horizon, remembering. "Sometimes he hit me a lot."

She turned her face toward his as the meaning of his words sunk in. "I'm sorry, Ben. I always figured you must have had a great father."

"I did. He *was* a great father eventually. But we had a pretty rough patch there for a while."

"What happened?"

"I told you about Mom dying when I was little?" He took a deep breath. "Dad didn't deal well with losing her. He couldn't get used to having me around instead of her. I think he must have started drinking, at first, to anesthetize his grief. Nicest person in the world when he was sober, but oh man, was he ever a mean drunk!"

"You're telling me the Petras I remember trying to protect me during the massacre was a mean drunk?"

"He was for at least part of my childhood. If Dad hadn't followed me into an empty church when I was trying to hide from him one Saturday night, I'd probably be ten times worse off now than Jack ever thought of being."

"But he stopped hurting you?"

"Finally. He got sober, realized what he was doing, and got help. He didn't have a choice." Ben chuckled. "The preacher threatened to whip him if he didn't."

"The *preacher* threatened him?"

"Paul Bascomb. He had a very short fuse when it came to dads who hurt their kids."

The memory washed over him, and it was as though he were there again—shivering, terrified, a little boy trying to make himself into a very small ball.

"Tell me."

Moriah's voice was so gentle; he wondered if this was the same woman who had been taking her anger out on nails a few moments earlier.

"There was an old church near our house that always kept its doors unlocked," he said. "Sometimes I would go there to hide. That's what I was doing when the new preacher found me. He saw me hiding beneath a pew, saw how terrified I was, and barely had time to process it all before Dad hit the door and came roaring in. I knew I was in for the beating of my life because, not only was Dad a mad drunk, he hated preachers and churches."

"What happened?"

"The most amazing thing. The preacher put his body between me and my dad and told him that he'd better not lay a hand on me."

"And your father listened to him?"

"Of course not. Dad loved a good fight, especially when he was drunk. He figured a preacher would be an easy knockout."

"Was he?"

"Nope." Ben grinned. "Dad had big hands, and he was very strong. I think he could have cold-cocked an elephant with those fists. He went after Brother Bascomb like an enraged bull, and even though I was just a little boy, I knew at that moment the preacher was going to die and I felt sorry for him."

"What happened?"

"Dad charged the preacher, and a second later, my dad was lying flat on his back, looking up at the ceiling."

"You're kidding!"

"Nope." Ben laughed. "Brother Bascomb had taught self-defense in the military before he became a preacher. Dad hardly knew what hit him."

"Then what?"

"After several more attempts to win the fight and several more times finding himself on his back, Dad got the message. He'd finally met a man he couldn't whip. The first, actually. Strangely enough, the respect he gained for the preacher that evening made him agree to get help. The preacher took me home to his family for a while, until Dad sobered up and made good on his promise."

"Why didn't the preacher just call Children's Aid?"

"You'd have to have known the man. It wasn't his way. He did things himself. And it worked. Dad started going to Alcoholics Anonymous, while meeting with Bascomb every week. One Sunday—I'll never forget this—I was sitting beside the preacher's wife, chewing on a stick of Juicy Fruit gum she had given me, and suddenly, here came my Dad, lumbering down the aisle. Only this time, he wasn't angry; he was sobbing. I'd never even seen him cry before. He changed his life that Sunday morning, gave it over to God, and never looked back."

"Never?"

"Nope. Not that I ever knew, and I probably would have known."

"So, there's hope for Jack?"

"There's hope for anyone."

"So how did he end up working at a clinic in the jungle?"

"He saw an article in National Geographic about a place called Machu-Pichu. That's a city famous for its ancient rock dwellings on a mountain in South America. As a stone mason, he became fascinated with the place. He wanted to study the techniques they used in ancient times. Finally, he went on a trip just to see it for himself. Kind of a reward, he said, to commemorate five years of sobriety."

"I've never heard of the place."

"A lot of people go there every year. I've been, too. I think you have to be a stonemason to truly appreciate it. Anyway, while he was there, he met a woman. She was a doctor, a missionary taking a little vacation from a clinic in the Amazon. When he called and told me about her, I was happy he had met someone. She sounded nice. My uncle had moved to the U.S., and I was living with him while Dad was away. I daydreamed that, maybe someday, Dad would bring home a mom for me."

"Did they get married?"

"No. I gathered from the letters he sent he had hopes they would, but she thought they needed more time together before taking such a big step. When he discovered there were others on their way to help build an addition to her small clinic, he volunteered to help. It was a win-win situation, he said. More time with her, and a way to pay God back for some of his bad years. After he got sober, my dad spent his few remaining years trying to make up for all the damage he had caused."

"And now you're translating the Bible for the exact same tribe that killed your dad."

"Yes."

"I still have a hard time wrapping my mind around that. I admire what you are doing, but I don't think I have it in me to forgive to that extent."

"Let me try to explain how it feels to me." Ben pointed out toward the lake. "Do you see your lighthouse standing out there?"

"You mean Nicolas's lighthouse?" There was a hint of sarcasm in her voice.

"Right."

"Of course, I see it. I've seen it every day of my life."

"How many ships do you suppose it saved during the years it was in service?"

"Hundreds," Moriah said, "maybe thousands."

"How many lives?"

"I don't know. I'm sure there were records kept of the wrecks and the people dredged out of the water, but it would be impossible to know all the ships and people who simply sailed safely on by. Why?"

"My life as a young boy was a nightmare, Moriah. Then everything changed. A light came on in the darkness of our house, much like the light your family kept going in that light tower for so many years. God's message changed my father completely and kept us from crashing into the rocks and sinking. It turned him from being a tortured animal that lashed out at everyone to being a man with joy and purpose. He became the father I'd dreamed of, a man who was kind to me all the time. Suddenly, I felt safe with him. More than safe. I felt *protected*. Something like that has a profound impact on a kid."

"I can understand why."

"There was one night, soon after he turned his life around, he borrowed a hymn book from the church. He sat by my bed with it and sang all the words to Amazing Grace. He had a good, deep voice. I was eight years old, and it became his nightly lullaby to me. He told me the words were talking about someone like him."

Ben stretched his hands out in front of him and flexed them.

"My father had big hands. Mine are a lot like them. I watched him take down men twice his size in bar brawls. I was so afraid of those hands. And then, suddenly, through the grace of God, those hands combed my hair and washed my face, tucked me in, and held hymn-books so that he could sing to me at night. I was twelve when he went to South America. My uncle, with whom I lived, was a lot older than my father, and his house was gloomy, but I went to school every day the proudest kid in that school. I told everyone my dad was a missionary, and they believed me because he sent me things from Brazil that my teacher displayed on a special shelf."

"But he never came back."

"He never came back. I cried for a while after he died and begged my uncle to let me go to him. I couldn't believe he was actually gone. When I was older, I still wanted to go to him, but in a different way. I studied hard, got a degree in linguistics, and found the tribe he was working with when he died. I figured, if God's word could turn a man like him into the man he became, it could change the hearts of the people who had killed him."

"Does Nicolas know all this?"

"No. Funny thing, if Dad and his mom had lived, we probably would have become stepbrothers. That's created a small bond between us, but I've not talked to him about my dad."

"Why not?"

"Partly because it's none of his business, partly because Nicolas is not the easiest man to talk to. I think that's one of the reasons he loves your aunt so much. They created a relationship when they were children that I don't think he's ever experienced with anyone else. He struck me as a very lonely, cold man the first time I met him. Since being here with Katherine, he's already different, happier."

"If they get married, I bet I'm going to have to live under the same roof with that man." There was sadness in Moriah's voice.

"You could come to the Yahnowa village with me, instead," he teased. "You could build me a new hut. I really need a new hut."

"What you need to do is help me finish this roof, so I'll be free to start work on the lighthouse."

"True. I'll help you. Then I need to start pulling a sermon together."

"A sermon?" Moriah asked. "Why?"

"While you were up here nailing shingles like you were killing snakes, your minister came around and asked me to speak for church next week."

"That should be interesting."

"I know." Ben said. "I can hardly wait to find out what I'm going to say."

Chapter Twelve

It had been several weeks since Moriah had been to church. It wasn't a matter of faith; it was a matter of having a business to run that took every spare minute preparing for and surviving tourist season. She was a lot better about showing up in the winter. This morning with Ben speaking, however, going to church took on a whole new significance.

She stood in front of her closet and pondered the fact that she owned nothing pretty to wear. It wasn't really that she was against nice clothes; it was just that her church had a very relaxed dress code—one that, fortunately for her, included jeans, t-shirts, and flannel shirts.

Most of the time, she didn't care all that much how she was dressed. Since she was constantly working at some sort of project, jeans, t-shirts, and flannels seemed good enough most of the time. But today, she had a yearning to wear a dress, a pretty one, something really nice that Ben would like.

Except she didn't have a pretty dress. All she had were a couple of okay ones that didn't fit all that well.

Without much hope, she reached into the back recesses of her closet and scooted all the clothes to the front.

A lone pantsuit appeared. It had been left abandoned in a closet in one of the cabins last fall. It was her size, so instead of putting it in their Lost and Found box, she'd had hung it here, ready to mail it off the minute anyone called to claim it, but thinking she might need it someday if no one contacted her about it. It had eventually gotten shoved to the back. She had forgotten all about it.

Pulling it out, she admired the rich fabric. It was a thin, creamy wool, perfect for a Sunday morning in spring. Why someone brought it along to a fishing camp, she had no idea. People did the strangest things, but she was grateful.

Then she slipped it on. The slacks fit well. The short jacket nipped in a little too much at the waist, but it would do. She carefully laid the jacket and slacks on her bed.

Rarely did she do anything with her straight hair, except wash and trim it with her aunt's sewing scissors. But this morning, she pulled it on top of her head, securing it with a ponytail holder.

There was a curling iron in her room she had experimented with a couple times and then abandoned as a waste of time. This morning, she heated it and attempted to create a cascade of tendrils like she had seen in a magazine. If her new hairstyle didn't turn out well, she figured she could always put it back in a braid.

She had never felt the need for much makeup, but she did have some lipstick she used on rare occasions. Carefully, she applied it on her lips, then rubbed just a little on both cheeks.

She put on her black dress flats, buttoned the jacket, and hurried down the hall to the bathroom, where there was a full-length mirror.

The image that greeted her was nothing like what she had hoped for. The black shoes looked awful with the pantsuit, the jacket was definitely too tight, and her hair simply wasn't going to work. It was too straight to stay in curls. She had been kidding herself even to try.

She trudged back to her bedroom, kicked off the black flats, and ripped the fastener from her hair. She unbuttoned the jacket and sat, dejected, on the side of the bed, contemplating her short fingernails and calloused hands. There was nothing she could do about them now.

This was what she got for telling herself she had too much work to do to care about her appearance. She couldn't even look nice when she really wanted to!

Ben would be here to pick her up for church in a half-hour, so she had to do something fast. She attacked her hair again and brushed it out straight. Maybe she would try something different. She pulled it into a low ponytail, and with great concentration and many bobby pins, she managed to fashion it into a semblance of a chignon.

There was an apricot-colored tank top she sometimes wore beneath her flannel shirts, so she put it on, then slipped the jacket over it, leaving it open. She checked the mirror in the bathroom again. Not too bad. She used a hand mirror to check the chignon. Actually, not bad at all. Kind of classy, actually.

Feeling a little better about things, she tried to figure out what to do about shoes. If only she had some that were a little fancier and a lighter color.

She thought back to the Lost and Found box. It was kept in the corner of the great room downstairs. She vaguely remembered a pair of light-colored low-heeled sandals being stored there.

Running down the stairs in her bare feet, she dug through the box, creating a pile of discarded games, books, clothes, shoes, bathing suits, goggles, sunglasses and… a pair of strappy, cream-colored sandals with a low heel. They were beautiful. And only a half-size too big.

"Please, God," she breathed and tried them on. She took a couple hesitant steps in her borrowed shoes and heard a low, heartfelt whistle.

"You look beautiful," Ben said.

Moriah whirled around and stifled a gasp. Ben was dressed for church, and Ben dressed up for church was something worth seeing.

He wore a white shirt, open at the throat, a dark charcoal tweed jacket, and light gray dress pants. There was something else different about him. She blinked.

"When did you get a haircut?"

"Yesterday evening. I found a barber in town. I was starting to scare myself when I looked in a mirror. I thought the people at church would prefer their speaker not to look like a wild man."

Moriah swallowed. "It's a nice haircut."

It was a great haircut. She could hardly believe the transformation.

"Are you ready, Moriah?" Katherine called from the top of the stairs. She was wearing a khaki shirtdress and was intent on fastening her watch. When she got it fastened, she looked up, stopped, and stared.

"What?" Moriah asked, defensively.

"I don't remember seeing you so dressed up for church before. Isn't that the outfit you found in Cabin Three's closet last summer?"

Moriah had always loved her aunt. She had always respected her aunt. But right now, at this moment, she wanted to strangle her aunt. Did Katherine *have* to tell Ben she had dressed in a guest's leftovers?

Ben turned to Moriah with a beatific smile. "You dressed up just for me?"

"No." Moriah raised her chin and shot a rebellious, hot glance at her aunt. "I just like to look nice once in a while."

Ben's smile faded a shade, but he made an effort to be gallant. "Looks like I'll be escorting the two most beautiful women on the island to church this morning."

"Correction. You'll be escorting one of the most beautiful women on the island to church this morning." Nicolas breezed through the door. He wore a black suit with a red-and-black striped tie and looked, to Moriah, like a lawyer ready to try a case, instead of a retired doctor or any man she had ever seen enter the door of their laid-back church. Nicolas was definitely going to stand out against the rumpled, casual clothing of the tourists and islanders who would be attending this morning.

"Kathy, my dear." Nicolas held out his arm as her aunt joined them. "Shall we go?"

"I'm sorry," Katherine whispered as she passed Moriah. "I should have thought before I said anything."

Moriah didn't have a chance to reply. As soon as Katherine put her hand inside the crook of Nicolas's arm, he led her out to the shiny, black Mercedes he had driven back from Toronto. Moriah watched as he opened the passenger side, tucked "Kathy" in, and closed the door after her.

Katherine didn't even look back as he whisked her away. It was the first time in twenty years Moriah and her aunt had not gone to church together.

"I noticed your aunt is not wearing buckskin today," Ben observed.

"Do you think Nicolas will change her too much?"

"For a while, maybe," Ben answered. "I don't think anyone can change someone else all that much, unless they want to be changed, especially someone your aunt's age."

"Katherine's only in her forties."

"Nicolas is robbing the cradle."

"That's not funny."

"Actually, it is." Ben stuck out his elbow in a parody of Nicolas. "Moriah, my dear, shall we go? It would appear that Nicolas and Katherine have forgotten us."

Moriah suppressed a giggle as Ben ushered her, with exaggerated self-importance, out to the resort truck. He opened the passenger door, removed a white handkerchief from his pocket with a flourish, laid it on the seat for her to sit on, and then closed the door

"Let Katherine have her day in the sun, Moriah," he said as he threw the truck into reverse. "Nothing you can say is going to make her stop caring about Nicolas, so you may as well try to enjoy her happiness."

Chapter Thirteen

When Ben pulled up in front of Jack's door, Moriah could barely believe her eyes. Jack was waiting for them, sitting on the steps of his house. He had on clean jeans and a pressed blue dress shirt. His wet, blonde hair still held the tracks of a comb.

Moriah scooted over, carefully dragging the handkerchief along beneath her. She hadn't thought, when she had donned the light-colored pantsuit, how dirty her truck might be. The last thing she wanted was to parade up the aisle in front of Ben with dirt stains on her backside. She eyed Jack's jeans enviously. Denim was so much less trouble.

Jack filled so much of the cab, she was forced to move close to Ben, which wasn't exactly a hardship. She enjoyed the intimacy of being pressed shoulder to shoulder with him. Briefly, she wondered if it were possible to become addicted to a scent. Ben always smelled of soap and sunshine, she analyzed, but there was that touch of spice there, too, something that made her think of jungles and exotic places.

"I appreciate you coming with us." Ben pulled back out onto the road.

"I had to think about it." Jack gazed out the side window, his head turned away from Moriah. "I only have to go to church twice to get the job, right?"

"That was the deal," Ben said, "plus, AA once a week all summer."

"I suppose going to church twice won't kill me."

"Hasn't killed me yet," Ben said.

They lapsed into silence the short distance to the church.

Moriah felt extremely self-conscious strolling in with the two men. Katherine was sitting with Nicolas in an entirely different place than usual. Since the church was already filling up, Moriah had to proceed almost to the front with Ben and Jack before they found a pew with enough room to accommodate the three of them.

She sat down and scooted over, while Ben ushered Jack in beside her and then chose the aisle seat. She didn't know if he was trying to make it easier to get up and go to the pulpit, or if he was trying to make certain that Jack didn't bolt.

"Ebenezer!" Howard Barrister, their preacher, had worked his way down the aisle greeting people. Now, he materialized beside them and pumped Ben's hand. "How's that truck running?"

"Fine. Thanks again for the use of your garage and tools."

"Hello, Moriah." The preacher nodded at her. "I couldn't believe it when Dr. Ebenezer McCain arrived at my doorstep. I've been following his work for several years. Fascinating. You and Katherine must be thrilled to have such a celebrity as a guest. And Jack Thompson, you are certainly a sight for sore eyes. Hope you enjoy the services."

As the preacher worked his way through the congregation greeting people, Moriah leaned forward and looked across Jack at Ben.

"Doctor?" she asked. "What's he talking about?"

Ben had the grace to look uncomfortable. "Just a Ph.D. in Linguistics. It's no big deal."

"You have a Ph.D. in Linguistics? Why didn't you tell me?"

Ben shrugged. "It never came up."

"Anything else you haven't told me?"

"I also have a Ph.D. in Biblical studies." Ben shrugged. "Sorry. School came easy for me, and I like to learn."

Services began with a prayer, and Moriah bowed her head, thoughts still whirling, trying to assimilate everything she had learned recently. First of all, with the exception of Jack, she seemed to be completely surrounded by people much more educated than her. Ben held a PhD, Nicolas was an M.D., and even Katherine had gone to medical school. All Moriah possessed in the way of formal education was a high school diploma and a certificate in carpentry from the local vocational school.

The prayer ended. She stared down at her hands, rubbing at her callouses, then she hid her hands beneath her thighs.

Jack glanced over and saw her hiding her hands—something he had chided her about since way back in high school. He pulled one work-worn hand out from under her thigh, held it in his, and gently smoothed out her fingers. Then he put her hand back onto her lap, patted it, and whispered, "Don't let it shake you—you're worth ten of him."

She straightened her shoulders, and folded her hands on her lap. Jack was right. She might not be worth ten of anyone, but she had come by those calluses honestly. No one could ever say she didn't work hard.

"We have a special guest with us this morning," Howard announced. "Dr. Ebenezer McCain is presently working on a translation for a tribe in the Amazon jungle. He'll be visiting our island for the summer. Would you care to say a few words to us now, Dr. McCain?"

Ben glanced apologetically at Moriah and then slowly got to his feet. There was a rustle in the church as the congregation settled, expectant and eager to hear someone new.

"The Yahnowa are historically a warrior tribe," Ben began.

With sinking heart, Moriah watched Ben turn into someone she didn't know.

His fine, deep voice rang with assurance. She saw people leaning forward as though to catch every word.

"In the recent past, Yahnowa manhood has been determined by kills. The worst thing a man could be called, the vilest cut he could be given, was to be called a 'no man killer'. Killing was their mark of masculinity, their recreation, their social status, and their life. We don't know how many tribes have become extinct throughout the ages solely because of intertribal warfare. This has begun to change, thanks, in part, to missionary efforts. Violet and Abraham Smith, a retired couple in their seventies, have worked with our tribe for many years. They were there when I arrived and have been instrumental in bringing about what peace exists in that area. The Yahnowa tribes are relieved by these changes. Like us, they prefer to live their lives and raise their children in peace."

Moriah found herself mesmerized, along with the rest of the congregation, by Ben's description of the living conditions of the people with whom he worked. One part of her listened, while another watched the man. Gone was the hesitancy she sometimes heard in his voice. Gone was the awkwardness he had often exhibited around her.

"But there are other concerns for these people of the rain forest. The greatest challenges today are the rapid deforestation by lumbering companies, the slash and burn farming practices, illegal gold miners, and the devastation brought by western disease—to which many of the more isolated tribes have no immunity."

"My personal efforts are a two-pronged approach. I am translating the New Testament into their language because I am convinced that the true applications of the teachings of Jesus can affect everything from marital relationships to intertribal friendships for the better. As I've become fluent in the Yahnowa language, I'm teaching the people, not only how to read and write their own spoken language, but how to communicate in the other languages with which they are surrounded, primarily Portuguese, Spanish, and English."

As he expressed his passion for the Yahnowa, he turned into a gifted speaker. It was obvious he loved the people with whom he worked.

"These Amazonian tribes survive by hunting, gathering, and gardening. The women tend gardens, where they grow as many as sixty crops. They also collect nuts, shellfish, and insect larvae. Wild honey is highly prized and the Yahnowa harvest fifteen different kinds. Men, women, and children all love to fish. Nutritionally, many of them have a better diet than we do. Although people think of them as primitive, much of their culture is enviable. For instance, no hunter ever eats the meat he has killed. Instead, he shares it among his friends and family. If he eats meat at all, it will be that which has been given to him from the kill of another hunter."

It was fascinating, but Moriah felt her heart drop with each sentence. Even though she had only known Ben for a short while, she had begun to daydream that he might choose to stay on the island after the lighthouse was finished. The jungles of Brazil had seemed far away, mystical, invisible, and therefore nonexistent. They seemed as unreal as the place names on the giant globe she kept in her room.

Ben leaned forward in his borrowed pulpit. "They have a huge botanical knowledge and use about five hundred different plants for food, medicine, and for building shelters. All of this is threatened by the factors I mentioned earlier. It is my belief that one way my skills can help them survive is to equip as many leaders of the Yahnowa as possible with the ability to communicate with government officials. My hope is to help them have a voice."

She had been so focused on the drama of the recent events in her own life she hadn't even begun to grasp the reality of his. This was not a man who would be content to live on this island, just as Nicolas had not been willing to give up his own freedom twenty years ago.

Her mind drifted back to the day on the roof when Ben had invited her to come to Brazil with him. They both knew he was joking, but she also knew he liked her. There was a spark between them she had never experienced before with any man. She also knew someone Ben's age needed a wife and was probably looking for one, but now, listening to him speak of his life's work, Moriah knew it couldn't be her. Unless...

Maybe she would try again. Maybe something within her had changed. Maybe knowing the truth about what she had been through as a child and understanding the reason behind the trauma would help her heal.

Unfortunately, crossing the bridge to the mainland was only part of the problem. She might manage to cross it, but could she ever get to the point she could also continue on to an airport, board a plane, fly to another country, live in such an alien environment?

No. She couldn't. The very thought of such a challenge made her chest hurt. Just the thought of it was enough to make her feel the beginnings of a panic attack. It was impossible. She could never do it.

Deliberately, like a surgeon incising a tumor, she cut away the fledgling thought of ever traveling with this remarkable man.

Ben finished his talk about his work with the Yahnowa and then sat down.

"Thank you, Dr. McCain," the preacher said. "That was very enlightening. Now, church, I think we need to pass the basket for a contribution to help him with his work..."

"Excuse me." Ben stood up. "That's very kind of you but no. The Yahnowa are not impoverished. They don't need western money. They have created what they need from the forest for hundreds of years."

"But you must need help with your own expenses," Howard said.

"Not really. I make more than enough to support myself." Ben sat down then stood up again. "I appreciate the thought, though, and thank you for the opportunity to speak."

"Will wonders never cease," Jack whispered to Moriah. "I like this guy, even if he did nearly drown me in my own shower."

"I think it's time to go," Ben said, jolting her out of her reverie after the church had sung a final hymn. She glanced around and saw people gathering their things and getting ready to go. A buzz of conversation filled the air.

Moriah dreaded working her way through the crowd today. Usually, she enjoyed talking to her friends, most of whom she had known since childhood. This morning, however, she didn't think she could carry on a lucid conversation with anyone. Ben was much more important than she'd ever dreamed. He was so far out of her league she could hardly believe he had been spending time with her. Already, he'd been taken over by a cluster of women from the church. Three of them were unmarried. Moriah averted her eyes.

Ben didn't belong to her, and he never would. It was time to toss that little daydream right out the window.

A lovely brunette made her way toward them, balancing a baby on her hip. Moriah snapped out of her emotional fog the minute she saw who it was.

"Hi," Alicia handed Jack the little girl. "Betsy has missed you."

Jack caught his daughter in his arms and nuzzled her neck. "I've missed her, too. And you." His voice caught.

Jack and Alicia had been in love with one another since high school. Moriah knew this as a fact. She had been there and watched. To think these two were having marital troubles was beyond sad.

"I'm surprised to see you here." Alicia fingered the lacy hem of her daughter's dress. "You never came when I asked."

Moriah waited for Jack to explain. When he didn't say anything, she felt compelled to step in. "We have this job for Jack over at the lighthouse and…"

Jack shot her a warning glance, and she stopped in mid-sentence.

"I'm sorry, Alicia," Jack said. "I should have come a long time ago, when you first asked me." He touched the brim of the tiny sunbonnet his daughter was wearing and rubbed a knuckle over her pink little cheek. "Can you trust me enough to start over?"

Moriah beamed at the couple.

"You'll stop drinking?" Alicia asked.

"I already have."

"Not a drop?"

"Not a drop, at least not since last week."

"You'll come to church with me?"

"It's not as bad as I expected."

"It's been really hard living with my mom, Jack." Alicia sighed with relief. "She's so bossy. I want my own husband and my own house and my own kitchen and my own stuff."

"About your stuff..." Moriah began. She was silenced, once again, by a look from Jack.

"Let's go home, Alicia." He turned to Moriah, dismissing her. "I'll see you Monday morning. Ben tells me we have a road to clear."

Moriah watched the tiny pink sunbonnet peeking over Jack's shoulder as the couple walked away. She couldn't help but smile when she heard Jack say, "About your kitchen, Alicia..."

"Are you ready to go?" Ben touched her arm.

"I guess so." Moriah was surprised he had extricated himself from the gaggle of women so quickly.

"Do you think we could go out the back way?" He eyed the crowd between them and the front door. "I don't want to turn down any more lunch invitations."

"You don't have to turn them down."

"Yes, I do."

"Why?"

"Because I want to have lunch with you." He steered her past the pulpit and out the back door. "Someone told me there's a really good restaurant in Little Current."

"We could go back to the lodge. Katherine usually puts a pot roast in the oven on Sunday mornings."

"You're looking forward to having lunch with Nicolas?"

"Good point. Lunch in Little Current sounds lovely. Nicolas and 'Kathy' would rather be alone, anyway."

"They do have wedding plans to make."

Moriah grimaced. "Don't remind me."

Chapter Fourteen

Ben had never felt prouder than he did standing beside Moriah as they waited in line at the old Anchor Inn Hotel in Little Current. The delicious aromas wafting in from the kitchen made him happy he was hungry. He couldn't wait to try whatever the special was today.

He loved the way Moriah had done her hair. Two wisps had escaped their pins on the drive here, and he was entranced as he stood behind her. The wisps danced upon her neck, moved about by a stray current of air.

This was the closest thing they'd had to a true date, and he was thrilled she had accepted. He was also happy Jack had gone home with Alicia, so he didn't have to share Moriah with anyone today. All in all, it had been a great day, so far.

He wondered if he might keep her out all afternoon—maybe a trip to the other side of the island, a walk along the far beach. It would be nice to stroll along the beach with her.

He had noticed the way she had looked at him while he was in the pulpit. He might be an amateur with women, but he would bet his new fishing rod that those green eyes gazing up at him were interested in more than just the information he was giving the people about the Yahnowa.

It was amazing that a woman like her would be interested in him, but he was pretty sure the signs were there. And, the best part of it all was that he had an entire summer to explore a relationship with her. He had high hopes she would be able to beat her problem about leaving the island. She was such a strong person. Certainly, she would be able to overcome such a little thing as driving over a bridge, especially now that she knew the reasons behind her phobia.

Ben was flooded with a sense of well-being as they waited for their table.

A young man with a bad complexion, a tattoo on each arm, and two small rings piercing his left eyebrow, stepped up to wait upon them. The piercings he sported didn't faze Ben. He had seen more impressive ones with the Yahnowa. He briefly pictured the boy decorated in paint and carrying a spear, and he chuckled. In spite of this boy's dangerous appearance, he would starve to death in the jungle if he didn't get eaten alive first.

"How many?" the young waiter asked, fingering his eyebrow ring as though to reassure himself it was still there.

Ben had seen the same gesture with Yahnowa, when the piercings were new and they had much on their mind. People were surprisingly the same, he had discovered, no matter where they lived. "Two." He drew out the word, savoring the taste of it on his tongue.

Two was such a nice number, he thought, as they followed the waiter to a small table beside a window overlooking the channel separating Manitoulin Island from the mainland.

Two was so much nicer than the number one. Not as nice as the number three, if the third was a little daughter or son. He felt a stab of envy thinking about Jack ambling out of church with that doll-baby of a little girl in his arms.

There were seasons in a man's life, Ben mused, as the waiter laid the menus on their table. Right now, he was in the season of wanting a family. For the past few years, even before meeting Moriah, he had yearned for a wife and child but had prepared himself to wait until the translation work was finished. Now, he wasn't at all sure he was willing to wait that long.

The waiter surprised Ben by gallantly drawing out Moriah's seat. Ben frowned. He had wanted to do that, and he doubted this particular waiter was always so solicitous. It was Moriah. She was beautiful, and her beauty wasn't lost on the waiter.

After they had been seated, she studiously scanned her menu while he studied her. Moriah's creamy, light-brown skin was flawless. Not one single freckle marred it, unlike him. The only way he could ever match Moriah's color was if all his freckles ran together.

Her hair, pulled back like it was, showed off the delicacy of her features. He flashed back to that moment, the first day, when he had brushed the dirt from her face while she was unconscious. She had the velvetiest skin he had ever touched.

Her lashes made delicate black fans on her cheeks as she gazed down, her fingers splayed, balancing the large menu. He loved her hands. They were so skilled, so competent. In the short time he had known her, he had seen them do everything from bait a hook to shingle a roof to cradle protectively a minutes-old baby. He would trust his life to those hands.

Moriah's eyes flicked toward the window, then she resolutely studied the menu again.

She glanced out the window again, realized he was watching, quickly closed the menu and laid it down.

"You ready?" The waiter materialized beside them with a stubby, yellow pencil poised over the order pad.

"I'll have the butter chicken," Moriah said. "What will you be having... Dr. McCain."

He gave his order. Another specialty. Pork chops with blueberry sauce. The waiter disappeared.

"I told you," he said. "School came easy for me, especially languages.

Having a couple doctorates isn't that big of a deal."

"I think it is a very big deal. My guess is that you worked harder than you let on. It couldn't have been easy." She folded her napkin into tiny pleats, still darting quick glances out the window.

"Of course, I worked. I had nothing else to do but work. My uncle died while I was still in undergraduate school. I had no family. All I had was a trade that paid a good wage and a goal."

"I'm proud of you for what you've accomplished." She smoothed her napkin onto her lap and stared out the window again, preoccupied with something outside. Ben wondered what it was she found so fascinating. There was nothing out there, except water and the bridge that connected the island to the mainland.

"Building a cabin from scratch and keeping a resort going is a pretty big deal, too," he said. "You've done that. You're an amazing woman, Moriah."

Once again, she simply stared out the window. Then suddenly, when he began to think she hadn't heard him, she faced him. "Do you see that bridge out there?"

He looked at the massive black iron structure. It looked like it had been built a hundred years ago, when sheer weight and mass equaled strength.

"I came across it when I arrived," Ben said. "Of course, I see it. Is that the one that has given you so much trouble?"

"I really can't cross it. A few months ago, I tried. Again."

"And?"

"Each time I try, my heart pounds so hard it feels like it's going to explode out of my body. My chest hurts. I can actually hear my heart beating inside my head. My body goes hot then cold. My legs and arms go numb. I can't get enough oxygen. It feels like—it feels like I'm dying."

"I'm sorry, Moriah." And he was sorry, but he simply could not imagine not being able to leave the island. Surely, there was some way for her to leave. If he were the one with the problem, he knew he would figure something out. "What about the ferry?"

"There is a long gangplank you have to cross to get on and off the Chi-Cheemaun. That's even worse because it's much narrower, and it sways and clanks. I've tried. It was really a lot of fun freezing on that gangplank in front of everyone. People behind me were waiting for me to move. Two men had to help carry me off because I was hyperventilating. No thanks. I won't be going through that again in this lifetime."

"Couldn't you just take your little fishing boat across?"

"Lake Huron is too dangerous to cross in a small boat, but I've taken it across here, at Little Current, beside the bridge. Do you know what's on the other side of the Little Current Bridge? Goat Island. Do you know what's on Goat Island? Not much. Do you know what's on the other side of Goat Island? Another bridge. And another island. And another bridge until eventually you arrive on the mainland, where, presumably, there will be more bridges. I don't do bridges, Ben. And the world outside Manitoulin Island is full of them. If we're going to be friends, it's only fair that you understand something—I really can't leave this island."

"I wish I could think of some way to help you."

"I wish I could think of some way to help me, too," Moriah said.

"Want to go try to drive across the bridge again?" Ben said. "Maybe it would be different with me cheering you on."

"It's not a baseball game. Having a cheerleader isn't my problem."

"Will you at least try?" Ben asked. "Maybe after we eat?"

"Okay." She sighed. "I'll try. But don't expect a miracle. I've tried so many times."

Chapter Fifteen

Katherine and Nicolas were not at the lodge when Moriah and Ben came home. She was grateful for that. Her attempt to cross the bridge had been disastrous. The minute they got home, Ben went straight to his cabin with a headache. She ran upstairs to her room, relieved not to have to deal with anyone after what had just happened.

She took off her pretty pantsuit, angrily kicked it into a corner, and then flopped onto her bed. She would never wear that silly outfit again. It would forever remind her of the moment she had resolved to give up any hopes of a future with Ben or anyone else who might want to live someplace other than Manitoulin Island.

The chignon bothered her. The hairpins pricked her scalp. She sat up again, plucked the hairpins from her chignon, and shook her hair out. How foolish she had been to try to look pretty this morning!

From now on, she would be the handyman and caretaker of Robertson's Resort. That's all. It was a good life. It was her life. It was the best life she could expect.

There was something wrong with her, and she didn't know how to fix it. The best thing she could do was cope the best way possible, just like she'd done her whole life.

Her attempt to cross the bridge after lunch with Ben had been ill-timed. By the time they drove to the bridge, it was almost two o'clock. That wouldn't have mattered for any other bridge in the world, except for the one at Little Current.

It was a swing bridge connecting the island with the mainland. It was old and built low. Many boats could not sail beneath it. So, every hour on the hour, during daylight, the bridge would swing a full fifteen degrees. Then it would stay like that for fifteen minutes so boats could pass through.

She and Ben got there just as the bridge began its slow movement out over the water. It didn't stop until it was completely parallel with the island.

They were the first in line to cross when it came back into position to accommodate the highway again, so she was treated to a front row seat of watching the heavy bridge move.

She had been geared up to try very hard not to disappoint Ben. The poor man was trying to help. But the longer she waited and watched, the worse her anxiety grew. Within the first five minutes of watching boats pass in front of them, she went into a full-fledged panic attack, which involved her begging him to get her away from there. It was difficult for him because there was a long line of cars backed up behind them. He had to maneuver the truck around while cars honked, and she went into a complete meltdown, crying and fighting for breath.

So very attractive. He'd probably make sure to avoid her for the rest of the summer.

Why did she have to be this way? When she knew absolutely there was no danger, why did her body keep reacting like someone was waiting to kill her if she set foot off Manitoulin Island?

As she lay there, another bit of memory floated to the surface for the first time...

"Quiet, little one," Karyona's daddy said. His hand still held firmly over her mouth. "Quiet like a little mouse."

Moriah was glad Akawe was holding her because she knew Mommy and Daddy trusted him. She was scared, but she trusted Akawe, too. Karyona's big brother, Rashawe, crouched as still and as deadly as a young panther in front of the door.

The screams stopped, and the five of them listened. Moriah knew Akawe wouldn't let her go to her mommy now. Even in her child's heart, she knew it was too late.

They sat like that for hours or, at least, it seemed like hours. As morning dawned, the villagers ventured out to see what was left of the clinic and the people, but Moriah was not allowed to go outside. Instead, the village elders crept to Akawe's hut, staring at Moriah as though she was a rare and unwelcome animal.

Moriah understood enough of the words they used to know the young warriors from Chief Moawa's tribe had killed all the white people at the clinic. Every last one of them were gone, except for her. Now, the village elders were discussing what to do with her.

Napognuma pulled Moriah away from Akawe, onto her lap, and nervously braided her hair while the elders discussed what to do. Karyona leaned against her mother's side and tightly grasped Moriah's hand.

"Little Green Eyes cannot stay," an elder said. "Chief Moawa hates the Jesus worshippers, and his tribe is more powerful than ours. He has many warriors, and we have few. He'll come for her when he hears a white child survived. There is danger for us if we keep her."

"This is true," Akawe said. "I have thought about this through the night. I think she should be taken to the convent school many mountains from here. The people there will know what to do with her."

"It is a very long way," the same elder pointed out, "and there are many dangers."

"I will have Rashawe." Akawe glanced proudly at his son, who stood silently, respectfully, near the doorway. "We will go together."

The elders nodded in agreement. "This is a good plan. Go swiftly. Before Chief Moawa remembers and returns to search for her."

When the village elders left, Napognuma bound Moriah tightly to Akawe's shoulders with strips of cloth. Then she handed him his spear and a parcel of boiled manioc.

"May our God go with you, my husband, and with you, little one." She kissed Moriah on the forehead as Akawe opened the door.

With Rashawe close behind him, Akawe started on a mile-eating trot through the forest that surrounded the village. Moriah glanced back at the charred clinic from which her parent's bodies had mercifully been removed. Her last memory of the village was seeing Karyona clinging to her mother's legs while they both waved good-bye.

The pain of remembering was too great. Moriah purposely shut it down. Was this the way things were going to be from this point on? Random, miserable, memories floating to the top, unbidden?

"Why do I have to be like this?" Moriah gritted her teeth against the emotional pain, the humiliations, the anger, all the disappointments. She jumped up from the bed and strode over to the giant globe and gave it a vicious spin. "Why can't I just be normal!"

Chapter Sixteen

Early the following day, Ben heard Jack coming long before he saw him. He heard the chug and rhythmic metallic thump of the bulldozer as it made its way down the road.

"Why didn't you use a trailer?" Ben shouted, when Jack rolled into the lodge's parking lot.

"It's got a flat. Figured it would be easier just to drive ol' Boss Hog on down here. It's not that far." Jack set the dozer's motor to a huffing idle, climbed out onto its metal tracks, then leaped down to the ground.

"You're ready to start?" Jack asked.

"Absolutely," Ben said. "Looks like you are, too. Doing okay?"

Jack smiled, white teeth lighting up a tanned face. "I'm still sober, if that's what you meant."

"That's what I meant. How are Alicia and the baby?"

"She's buying new dishes today," Jack admitted. "I spent a big part of last night doing the final clean up. We're going to be okay. We have to be. I won't lose my wife and baby girl again. Once was enough."

Ben appraised the handsome giant. Today, by the grace of God, Jack was sober. Now to keep him that way. He would pray, of course, but he knew work was especially valuable when a man had private demons to fight. Many times, he'd seen good pay attached to honest labor go a long way toward getting a person back on track.

"You can tell where the old road bed is, right?" Ben shaded his eyes with both hands as he scanned the line of new growth trees. The sun was bright through the early morning mist.

"I've lived here my whole life, Ben. I know exactly where the road bed is."

"Do I need to get a chainsaw crew in there first?"

"Nope. Boss Hog and me can move everything out of the way, no problem." Jack patted the huge dozer affectionately. "In two days, you'll be driving over a road so smooth you'll think you're driving on silk."

"As long as we can get through." Ben wasn't impressed with Jack's boasting. In fact, he considered it a bad sign. Men who truly did good work didn't have to brag about it; they let the work speak for itself.

Jack mounted his dozer, pulled it out of idle, and then roared off toward the mouth of the old roadbed, which lay at a right angle to the resort's private driveway.

The two properties were so linked it was probably just as well Nicolas and Katherine were going to get married. Otherwise, there could be some major property disputes.

As Jack began to cut a swath through the scrubby pines, Ben went in search of Moriah to make sure she'd made it through the night okay. He was upset with himself for trying to talk her into crossing the bridge yesterday. How arrogant he had been, as though being with him would provide some sort of magic elixir that would make it possible. Watching her experience a full-scale panic attack had been disturbing, but it had also convinced him her pain was real. As silly as her phobia had seemed to him at first, Moriah wasn't playing games. Her fear of leaving her island went deep.

Chapter Seventeen

He found Moriah and Katherine standing on the path in front of Cabin One. They were watching a pair of new running shoes attached to skinny, denim-clad legs, which were sticking out from a hole in the foundation.

"The snake man from the reservation is here." Moriah said, staring intently at the running shoes. "He just now crawled in after them. The only tools he has with him are a pair of gloves and a gunny sack. He's my new hero."

"Shhh," Katherine said.

A high-pitched quivery singsong wafted out from beneath the cabin.

"That must be a native snake-charming song he's using." Moriah's voice was filled with awe.

As Ben listened to the chant, he thought it sounded strangely like "Achy Breaky Heart." At least it did to him, but he was no judge of First Nation snake songs.

The shoes slowly emerged, then the legs and body of a tall, slender man. He wore a red cowboy shirt tucked into faded blue jeans. His hair was white and hung in two long, thin braids. Deep wrinkles creased his cheeks, and intelligent, brown eyes looked out from deeply recessed sockets. His running shoes were at odds with the rest of him. They were obviously new and expensive-looking.

"It was a small den. There were only eight," the snake man said, holding a squirming burlap bag in his leather-gloved hands.

"Eight?" Moriah moved several feet away from the writhing sack. "There were *eight*?"

"Sam Black Hawk." The old man drew off one glove with his teeth and reached out to shake Ben's hand.

"Ebenezer McCain." Ben was surprised by the strength of the man's grip. "Thanks for taking care of the snake problem."

"These? These snakes are not a 'problem.' They are beautiful specimens. In fact, two of the females are gravid."

"Gravid?" Moriah hugged herself, nervously rubbing her arms with her hands.

"Filled with young."

"You mean we almost had baby snakes?" Moriah edged a couple more feet away from the sack.

"In a few weeks, yes. There could have been as many as forty young beneath your cabin. Of course, they would not have all stayed there. They have to hunt to live, and there are not enough mice under one cabin to support such a large community of reptiles."

"Thank goodness you came!" Moriah danced in place as though in a hurry to leave. "I'll go get the checkbook. How much do we owe you?"

"Are you all right, Sam?" Katherine looked closely at the old Ojibwa. "They didn't strike at you, did they?"

"Today is the exact right temperature for capturing Massasaugas. Cool enough to make them slow and sluggish, not cold enough for them to go back underground. The pregnant ones, they cannot move so fast, anyway. Do you want to see?"

"No. No. That's okay," Moriah protested.

"But they are beautiful." Black Hawk slipped his leather glove back on and opened the mouth of the sack. His hand darted in and came out grasping a writhing snake just behind the head. "Here, hold this." He handed the bag to Ben. "Do not hold it against your body, though," he warned, "or lay it on the ground."

Ben held the sack carefully at arm's length. He wasn't particularly afraid of snakes—it would be impossible to make a living as a stonemason and be too fearful of the creatures that so frequently lay beneath the stones. But he wasn't particularly fond of them, either.

"You have a terror of rattlers?" The old man focused on Moriah.

"I *hate* snakes!" Moriah admitted. "I don't know why God ever made them in the first place."

"I do not pretend to know the mind of God," the old man said, "but I know this—he made them with great care. Come closer, daughter. I will hold this little mother-snake carefully so she cannot bite. Let me show you this miracle God made."

Ben's arm was already getting tired holding the bag straight out from his body. Who would have guessed a few rattlers would be so heavy? Gingerly, he switched arms as Moriah carefully approached the old man.

"That is good. You are a brave woman to fight your fear," Sam said, "and a wise one to keep your wits about you and to crawl so slowly away when you were under the cabin. A rattler will not strike at body heat that moves slowly. It is used to prey that runs away quickly. Moving slowly confuses it."

As though mesmerized, Moriah crept a few inches closer to Black Hawk as he held the snake's head firmly in his gloved hand, supporting the rest of it with the other. Over two feet of snake stretched between the man's gloved hands.

"You should touch this little snake now," Black Hawk said. "Touch it while you're completely safe, and let your fear leave you."

"I don't think I can." Moriah's hands were jammed deep into her pockets.

"Some people think snakes are slimy, but they are wrong. The skins are smooth and dry. It will feel like satin beneath your fingertips, and you will carry that feeling with you the rest of your life. It will help take away some of the fear."

Ben watched as Moriah visibly struggled with herself. She was trembling as she slowly stretched out her hand—then jerked it back as though from a burning coal. She took a deep breath, reached out a second and third time, quickly yanking her hand back before touching the snake.

"You can do this, daughter," the old man said. Once again, he began to sing softly the wild, high-pitched song that had drifted earlier from beneath the cabin.

Whether or not it affected the snake, Ben would never know, but it seemed to give Moriah heart. She reached out a steady hand this time and touched the snake without jerking back. She stroked it. Once. Twice.

"Look at her face, daughter; see the little black mask she wears across her eyes? She is trying to fool you into thinking she is a robber, a bandit. She thinks she is fearsome, wearing this mask. But she is only a little mother-to-be, who is hungry and wishing this old man would let her loose, so she could go running into the grass to find a nice fat mouse to fill her belly."

"She does feel like satin." Moriah smiled hesitantly up at Black Hawk.

"Would you like to hold her? I can show you how, so she cannot bite."

Moriah jammed her hands deep into her pockets and took two steps backward. "Nope. I think that's all I'll do today."

"You have done well. Now that you have seen a Massasauga up close, you will never have to be afraid of any other snake you see on Manitoulin."

"Why not?"

"Because the Massasauga is the only one on our island with venom. All the others are harmless. You may play with them if you want."

"I don't think I'll be playing with snakes any time in the near future,"

Moriah said, her hands now twined behind her back.

"That is just as well, because they are shy animals who prefer to be left alone."

"What will you do with these?" Katherine asked.

"They are very territorial, so I must take them far away to keep them from returning. I will take them by boat over to Lonely Island. There are so many Massasaugas on that island eight more will not make a difference."

He deftly thrust the snake into the sack Ben held, then quickly closed and twisted the neck.

"Would you mind carrying this to my truck, my son?" Black Hawk asked. "It is a long way for an old man to walk with a heavy sack."

"Of course, I'll be happy to help."

"What do I owe you?" Moriah asked. "I want to pay."

"For *your* family? Nothing. You have done much for us already. It is good to give something back."

"Thank you," Katherine said, "more than you can ever know."

Ben watched Moriah and Katherine chatting together as they walked back to the lodge. Moriah didn't seem to be too traumatized by her meltdown yesterday, and he was relieved.

He turned back to Black Hawk, who'd pulled a handkerchief out of his pocket and was tying it around his left arm.

"Give me that bag before you drop it and hurt them," Black Hawk commanded. His voice had changed, grown stronger, lost some of the old man quaver. Ben handed him the bag, which Black Hawk grabbed easily with his right hand. He then lifted the back of his hand to his mouth for a moment, sucked, spit, and headed toward his truck, which was parked in back of the cabins.

"I thought it was too heavy for you to carry so far," Ben protested, following him.

"Don't be ridiculous. I could hike to the other side of the island and back with it. I run marathons, McCain. The only reason I wanted to drag you into this was because I wanted a chance to talk with you alone about Moriah."

"You run marathons?" Ben was amazed.

"I placed first in Canada's over-seventy senior's division this year," Black Hawk said. "But that's not what I wanted to…"

"That's the reason for the new running shoes!"

"What did you expect? Beaded moccasins? Yeah. I have to buy a new pair every five hundred miles. It's kind of like getting new tires; the old ones wear out."

"Have you always run?"

"No. I started in my sixties. At first, it was an excuse to get away from the grandchildren and great-grandchildren. They all live close to us, and sometimes, they about drive me nuts." He preened a little. "Also, my wife likes for me to be buff."

Ben's mind was reeling from the sudden change in the man's personality. "What about all that mumbo jumbo back there, the chant, the 'courage, daughter' stuff."

"You liked my chant?" Black Hawk chuckled. "The Ojibwe do have a snake dance that is supposed to be healing. It mimics the shedding of skin and all that stuff. It's very impressive, but if we have a chant for pulling snakes out from underneath a cabin, I never heard of it. I just make 'em up so people think I've got something mystical going on. It seems to keep everyone calm."

"It doesn't have any effect on the snake?"

"Of course not," Black Hawk said. "Snakes aren't Billy Ray Cyrus fans. At least, Massasaugas aren't. I'm not sure about the others."

"So that *was* 'Achy Breaky Heart' you were singing!"

"Don't tell Moriah. She needed confidence; the song helped. Don't argue with success, McCain."

"All that was a show for Moriah?"

"Of course, it was. She went through a terrible ordeal beneath that cabin. I wanted to help her get over it if I could."

"Are you really a snake expert," Ben said, suspiciously, "or are you pretending about that as well."

"Certified herpetologist. I have a B.A. in Zoology." Black Hawk grabbed a piece of twine from the back of his truck and tied the bag closed. "Class of '57.' I milk Massasaugas for venom and sell it to laboratories so they can make antivenin—which, by the way, I could use some of right now."

"What do you mean?"

Sam Black Hawk stripped off his leather gloves and sucked at the back of his hand again. He spit then audibly sighed at Ben's ignorance as he leaned against the tailgate of the truck. "Rattlesnakes have a limited amount of venom—so they control the amount they put in their victim—using just the tiniest amount to paralyze a mouse, for instance, until they can digest him. The reason they hold back is because, if they use up all the venom at once, they'll have to go hungry for a few weeks until their bodies replace it."

"What does that have to do with you needing antivenin?"

"Moriah was in mortal danger under that cabin. Rattlesnakes never have as much venom as when they've just come out of hibernation. It's all built up. Had she tried to get out of there quickly, making it possible for them to track her body heat, they would have struck at such a large target with all the venom at their disposal. She would have died. Painfully." He reached into his pants pocket. "Here," he said, tossing his truck keys to Ben. "You drive."

"You didn't answer the question."

Black Hawk cinched the handkerchief more snugly around his arm.

"One of those Massasaugas managed to give me a little 'kiss' while I was beneath the cabin. I think it might be a good idea if we headed for the hospital."

The old man's face was beginning to turn gray as Ben spun gravel all the way out of the parking lot.

Black Hawk glanced at Ben before closing his eyes. "Don't you dare tell Moriah about this."

Chapter Eighteen

Ben waited at the hospital until Black Hawk's hand had been put in ice, the wound had been cleansed, bandaged, and a shot of antivenin administered. The bite was light, they said. No venom had reached his heart.

"I just hate it when that happens," Black Hawk complained as Ben helped him climb back into the truck.

"Getting bit?"

"Yeah, I really hate snakes."

Ben stood on the brakes. "But you're a herpetologist!"

"I know." Black Hawk sighed. "Ain't it a mess?"

As Ben began driving again, Black Hawk explained, "Being a First Nations male, who is terrified of snakes, is embarrassing. I first studied snakes to get over the fear, and by the time I'd gotten over the fear, I was too fascinated by them to leave them alone."

"But you just said you hated them."

"I never said it had to make sense." He adjusted the bandage on his hand. "I was pretty good back there with Moriah, though, wasn't I?"

"You were great."

"I hear you and she are going to be restoring the lighthouse."

"News gets around fast. How did you find out?"

"Would you believe drums?"

"I don't think so."

"How about smoke signals."

"Nope."

"Would you believe Katherine called me on my phone and told me?"

"Yes. That I would believe."

"Is it true? Are you going to restore it?"

"Looks like it. Jack began putting in the road today, so we can start getting supplies to it."

"This will probably come as a surprise to you, but Moriah's grandfather was my second cousin, as well as my blood brother."

"I don't think anything you could say right now would surprise me, Black Hawk. But that blood brother stuff, do you guys still do that?"

"With the possibility of AIDS and Hepatitis C and STD's? Are you kidding? No way. But back when we were kids and the world felt pure, it still seemed like a good idea. It was hard on me when he died. I miss my old friend badly some days."

"I can imagine." Ben slowed down as he crossed the bridge onto Manitoulin. "By the way, where am I taking you?"

"Back to Katherine's lodge. I'll drop you off. I feel fine now. I can drive myself home from there."

"Are you sure?"

"Yes, I'm sure. I'm the snakebite expert, remember? Besides I have to take those snakes over to Lonely Island. We still got eight rattlers in the back of this truck."

"Why don't you take them home and milk them or whatever you do."

"I've already got more than enough. These islands are crawling with Massasaugas."

"Then why are they on the endangered species list?"

"I don't know. Makes the government feel important, I guess." Black Hawk fingered the bandage on his hand again. "McCain?"

"Yes."

"Are you going to restore the lighthouse completely?"

"As close as possible."

"Even the tower?"

"Especially the tower. Moriah wants to put a big telescope there and a beacon."

"I thought maybe she was thinking about putting the light back in."

"Someone stole the lens a long time ago."

"I know. I remember. But if she had a true Fresnel lens, do you think she would put it back in?"

"She says it's not possible to buy a new one, and the old ones are either in museums or private collections."

"Hypothetically speaking," Black Hawk said, "do you suppose the Coast Guard would press charges if the lens accidentally turned up?"

"I have no idea. Hypothetically speaking, could the lens possibly still be in good shape?"

"The lens could hypothetically be in excellent shape."

Black Hawk pulled the bandage off his hand and stuck it in his pocket as Ben pulled into the resort parking lot.

"Darn thing was bothering me," Black Hawk said.

"I noticed." Ben climbed out of the truck, leaving the keys dangling in the ignition. "When the tower is finished, I'll give you a call."

"No need." Black Hawk scooted behind the wheel. "I'll already know."

Chapter Nineteen

....

One week later, Moriah surveyed the fresh road to the lighthouse and nodded in appreciation. She was proud of Jack. He might have a few personal issues, but he was a world class heavy equipment operator. He'd done a great job, just like she had expected. Things with that little family of his was getting back on track as well. So far so good.

"Not bad," Ben said. "Are you ready to start?

The earthy scent of freshly turned dirt and uprooted tree roots filled the air. The road was as straight and level as a gun barrel, with the lighthouse centered at the end.

"I am. This week will be a little frantic, but I think we've finally got things under control. Nicolas has been following Katherine around like a puppy, helping wherever he can. I actually saw him mopping the kitchen floor this morning. Plus, I hired Alicia part-time to take care of helping with reservations and greeting people as they show up. She can do that and still take care of little Betsy."

"Is it always so busy the first week of tourist season?"

"Yes, and it pretty much stays that way. Once the Chi-Cheemaun starts bringing in tourists, it always gets a little crazy. We'll usually get a few like the Wrights and Camilla's family, who drive in from the north over the Little Current bridge so they can get here early, but it's when the ferry starts running that the season truly begins."

"Do you enjoy doing this for a living, Moriah?" he asked.

"I never really thought about it. It's all I've ever known. Seems like I've spent most of my life either preparing for or recuperating from the day the ferry starts bringing the usual crush of summer travelers up from Tobermory on Bruce Peninsula, to South Baymouth here on the island. A large part of our population earns the bulk of our yearly income in the space of these next three months."

"It sounds intense."

"It is."

She doubted Ben had any idea how intense it could get. Guests would begin arriving at all hours of the day and night, bringing with them pleas for extra linens, dishes, and folding cots. Concerns about plugged toilets, mice, and cranky cook stoves were a daily chorus to which Moriah automatically responded. She had grown up with it. She dispensed advice on everything from the best fishing spots to an occasional on-the-spot family intervention when frayed tempers flared.

Except, this year, she would be doing it while attempting to restore her lighthouse.

Nicolas's lighthouse, she corrected herself.

Although, now that Katherine was back in his life, Nicolas seemed content to give Moriah and Ben complete freedom with the restoration. Unless Moriah was mistaken, he seemed to have lost all interest in the place. Perhaps that was because he had a new goal—moving into the lodge with Katherine.

That would be rather awkward for her, but Katherine was half-owner of the resort. If she wanted to marry Nicolas and let him move in with her, then that's the way it would be.

"What do you think, Moriah? Can we do it?" Ben nodded toward the derelict lighthouse.

She looked at him, studying his sturdy build, his determined eyes, his capable hands. There was something about Ben that increased her confidence and strength and made the horrific jungle flashbacks she continued to have almost bearable.

"I think, together, we can do just about anything we set our minds to, McCain."

Chapter Twenty

"We'll dismantle it, stone by stone." Ben peered through the camera he had brought with him as he circled the light tower, snapping pictures from all sides. "The stones will have to be taken down, one at a time, numbered, and re-laid after the new foundation is poured. I'll use that inner wall in the old office to mount these photos, so we can reference them easily."

"We need to start assembling a crew," Moriah said.

"Besides Jack, who do you know?"

"I've had a mental list of my dream team for restoring the lighthouse for about two years now."

"Get them. Just make sure I've got a couple of your most dependable people with me on that tower. Will Jack be one of the guys you hire for that, or does he take on work besides heavy equipment?

"Jack's pretty good at everything. I think he'll jump at the chance for more steady employment this summer."

"I'll need some real muscle beside me when we begin to dismantle the tower." Ben shot a picture of the outside of the cottage. "I think Jack would have the strength."

"I'm sure he would."

"I know it's none of my business," he moved over a few paces and clicked a picture of the broken foghorn room, "but did you and he ever have a thing?"

"A thing?"

"Like back before Alicia."

"Me and Jack?"

"Yes, you and Jack. The man resembles a Greek god when he's cleaned up and sober," Ben said. "And you've always been friends. I figured maybe…"

"A thing?"

"You know, in a romantic way."

Moriah was surprised. "We grew up together, Ben. No, he's always just been a friend."

Ben studiously kept his eyes on the viewfinder of the camera. "I'm glad."

Moriah's heart melted. Apparently, Ben was still interested in her, in spite of her limitations. After that meltdown at the bridge, she was surprised he hadn't run screaming back to Brazil. She hoped this summer went well. If he really learned to like the island, maybe he would consider living here on the island and make trips back to the Amazon, instead of the other way around.

"I don't want anything to happen to you or to Jack," she said. "Is taking down that tower going to be as dangerous as I think it will be?"

"Yes." Ben didn't hesitate. "It will be."

In spite of the lurch in her stomach at his words, she appreciated the fact that he was not candy-coating the danger. It showed her that he was truly seeing her as an equal in this job.

"Then we'll need plenty of freestanding scaffolding on the outside of it," she said. "Metal, not wood. I might need to have it special-built. Do you plan to work exclusively from the outside?"

"I don't think anyone should be within that tower during the dismantling. After the new foundation has cured and we begin to rebuild, it will be safe to work inside. I'm figuring I'll concentrate on the tower if you are comfortable being in charge of the cottage and foghorn room. Does that work for you?"

"Let me see." Moriah took stock. "I'll need new timbers for the roof, new insulated windows, new slate tiles. I'll keep the antique locks and hinges. They'll need to be scrubbed and oiled. The moisture from the lake eventually ruins anything metallic…"

"Hold on." Ben pulled a small notebook from his pocket. "Let me make a list."

"The walls need to be scraped clean of about a hundred years of peeling wallpaper. Those wooden floors in the kitchen, where all the rain has come in, will have to be replaced. The rotten linoleum has to go. Maybe, I can find some that matches it. I liked that floral pattern, and it would lend an air of authenticity. I'll check into wallpaper patterns from the 1800's, as well. I'll need to install bathrooms, in addition to plumbing the kitchen. Everything will have to be wired, not to mention putting in some form of central heat. Of course, I'll keep the potbellied coal stove and fireplace for authenticity."

"You sure you're up for all that?" Ben asked.

She squared her shoulders and lifted her chin. "Piece of cake, McCain."

Ben draped an arm around her shoulders.

"The girl of my dreams," he said with utter sincerity.

The big problem was figuring out what to do about it.

Chapter Twenty-One

During the next few weeks, the tip end of the small peninsula, where the lighthouse stood, took on the appearance of a tiny, bustling village.

By the time Moriah managed to get her team assembled and the work had begun, nearly everyone on the island had heard the news of the restoration.

A good number of the older Manitoulin residents seemed intent on watching. It seemed to be high entertainment for the elderly. Many came day after day, bringing folding chairs with them. Now that the road was open, it was easy access as long as the weather held. Quite a few packed a lunch.

These ancient owners of stories and memories chatted about storms and rescues, while craning to see everything. Some spoke with nostalgia about the picnic parties her grandparents had held there so long ago.

Each story felt like a gift to Moriah, a treasure she stored in her heart. She was inspired by the fact that her family's dedication had meant something, not only to the ships where lives and cargos had been saved, but to the community, as well.

"You swing a hammer just like your daddy, Missy," an older gentleman said as he watched her replacing a rotten windowsill. He was dressed in a well-cut dark suit and leaned on a gold-headed ebony stick

She was distracted by her work. The board she was nailing was a smidgen short. She had measured carefully, but mistakes happened when a carpenter got tired. Reluctantly, she pried up the board and threw it on the scrap pile. It was time to call it quits for the day.

"Let's pack it in, men!" she called, gathering her tools. "Time to go home." Only then did she realize she had been rude to the old man. "I'm sorry, sir. What did you say?"

"I said you swing a hammer just like your daddy." He smiled. "You're the spitting image of him."

It felt good to hear that phrase again after all these years. "You think so?"

"It's a fact." The old man took a step closer. "I remember coming here one day when you were just a tyke, not much more than three or four years old. Your daddy was doing some repairs, and you were toddling around behind him, wearing a little bitty tool apron. I went home and told my wife all about the little carpenter's daughter. Cutest thing I ever saw."

Moriah noted the kindness in the gentleman's eyes and was grateful for the gift of memory he was giving her.

"I remember very little about my father, and I don't remember the tool apron at all. Are you sure?"

He nodded. "He said your mother had made it. Your daddy was a wonderful carpenter and a good man. It was obvious how much he loved you."

Moriah's throat swelled with emotion at the man's words. "Thank you. I appreciate you taking the time to tell me that."

"You're welcome." He glanced over at the partially deconstructed light tower with its necklace of metal scaffolding. "It's an important thing you're doing here. I'm certain your father and grandfather would be proud of you."

Moriah smiled. "You think?"

He nodded. "We all are. Everyone one on the island is proud of what you're doing here. A piece of our heritage was nearly gone, but you and Jack and that stone mason fellow are bringing it back to life. Thank you."

Moriah watched as the old man limped back to where a driver and car were waiting. He waved briefly before the driver backed away.

"Do you know who that was?" Jack asked

"I have no idea."

"Isaac Jones. He used to be a ship captain back when your grandfather manned the lighthouse. I was talking to him earlier."

"Did he tell you anything else?"

"A bit." Jack grinned. "Just the small fact that your grandfather saved his life and several of his crew."

"Oh wow. I wish I'd known."

"Don't worry about it. He told you what he came to say; that you're doing something important here." Jack gazed about them at the sturdy crew of workers packing up their tools. "I have a feeling we all are."

Chapter Twenty-Two

Even with the lighthouse requiring all of her and Ben's attention and with tourist season heavy upon them, Nicolas and Katherine managed to find time to plan an August wedding. Fancy invitations went out in the mail, and catalogs of wedding finery piled up around Katherine's favorite chair.

Nicolas surprised everyone by rolling up his sleeves and doing an excellent job, not with the lighthouse, which he rarely visited, but with the running of the resort. He donned his khaki shorts, a t-shirt emblazoned with the words "Robertson's Resort," and seemed utterly content. Moriah even came upon him once as he hung freshly laundered sheets on the line. To her astonishment, the man was whistling.

In the evenings, when Moriah came back to the lodge, she noticed her aunt was softening into a younger-looking, much happier version of herself. Katherine's expression was no longer that of stoic acceptance. Instead, she smiled more often, her eyes lit up at the smallest things, and Moriah had heard her humming as she cooked. Moriah knew that Nicolas was the cause of that new happiness, and she was grateful.

In spite of the upset Moriah had experienced earlier, her days now fell into a seamless rhythm and routine as she, Ben, and the crew worked together. Stone upon stone, bracings and chisels and rock dust, roof trusses and fresh new flooring, it was exhilarating to see her dream coming together.

Moriah loved the feeling of straining her muscles to the maximum each day alongside the company of the workmen, eating a quick sandwich with her back braced against the shady side of the cottage, then swigging down the icy water from the newly restored well and outdoor hand pump. Ben often came to sit beside her in the shade of the cottage for a few minutes to figure out some small challenge that might have arisen. She appreciated the fact that he respected and valued her opinions. Then, they would swing back into the task at hand, renewed.

It was the happiest she had ever been in her life.

Each day, some satisfying portion of the restoration was accomplished. Each evening after supper, Moriah stood in a hot shower, soaking her sore muscles. Then, she would put on clean clothes and meet Ben, who always waited for her on the back-porch swing. They'd spend at least an hour each night in the privacy of the swing, talking about their day, planning the next. It was the best part of the day.

Later, Moriah would crawl into bed, exhausted. Each morning, she awoke looking forward to the day with eager anticipation. Much of that eagerness was in looking forward to seeing how much they would accomplish that day, but some of it was knowing she would get to see Ben again.

Neither of them spoke about what would happen when the summer ended. They were careful with each other, holding back, determined to continue to maintain their friendship, knowing that saying too much too soon could destroy it.

No matter how early she rose, however, Ben was always in the lodge's great room a bit earlier, working on his translation. He insisted he was so used to working in a village with a dozen children underfoot that he felt lonely working in his cabin.

Neither Nicolas nor Katherine brought up all that had been said the day of her nightmare out at the lighthouse, the day of the thunderstorm.

Everyone skirted around the issue, avoiding it, all four of them almost too busy to breathe. They had no time to delve into the issue, so they left it alone. They all seemed content to wait for her to bring it up if she wanted to, and she chose not to.

After the restoration of the lighthouse was accomplished, after the last guest had left, after she had buttoned up the cottages and prepared them for winter, then she and Katherine would have months to sort things out. Winter often felt never-ending this far north. There would be plenty of time then to talk.

For now, she was grateful they left the subject alone. Now that she understood the reasons Katherine had fabricated a different reality for her all these years, she craved time to sort things out in her mind, especially since bits of memories kept trickling into her conscious, triggered by simple, everyday things.

One day at the work site, while wiping her forehead with the blue-patterned work handkerchief she kept in her pocket, she abruptly had an image of her mother in the jungle, tying her hair up off her neck with one exactly like it.

A child's wooden toy left on the path in front of the cabins suddenly dredged up a picture of Petras whittling out clumsy little tigers and monkeys for her and the other children in the village.

But images of the massacre kept creeping in, too. Her child's impressionable mind had apparently taken a photographic snapshot of those moments and then tucked that snapshot away until she was old enough to look at it. She could now recall, with accuracy, even the clothes her parents had been wearing.

She dealt with this hodge-podge of rediscovered mental pictures the best she could. Sometimes, while she worked, she fit pieces together in her mind, making new discoveries every day. Many things made sense to her now.

For the first time, she understood why she had always struggled with a low-grade sadness, so different from the other children growing up on the island. For the first time, she realized that, along with the four lives that had been taken during the massacre, four other innocent lives had been nearly destroyed. The trauma wasn't hers alone. Ben, Katherine, and Nicolas had suffered, also.

Ben had pieced together a life by devoting himself to the very tribe where his father had met his death. But even Ben was not entirely whole. He still mourned the father he had come to love so much.

Katherine had sacrificed marrying the man she loved and her dream of becoming a doctor in order to care for a damaged niece. Moriah now realized just how seldom she had ever seen her aunt smile. She suspected that competent, wise Katherine had been as sad as Moriah, until Nicolas, with all his faults, stepped in.

And Nicolas. Ah, Nicolas. A gifted medical student when his mother died, he had given up his dream of becoming a surgeon by incomprehensibly taking on his mother's profession of obstetrics, a specialty Moriah felt certain he was emotionally ill-suited for. She found herself wondering, sometimes, if his hasty and poorly chosen marriage might have been the worst fate of them all.

Then, there was herself. Moriah wished she could go back in time, take the silent little girl she had once been, and hold her in her arms. Her heart swelled with pity for that little girl, pity for all of them, crippled, yet in their own way, valiant. They had all tried so hard to put the pieces back together and make lives for themselves.

As Moriah's hands sawed and hammered, her mind imagined their separate lives integrated into a jigsaw puzzle, scattered onto the floor by Chief Moawa's violent hand. Then, she imagined God patiently picking up the pieces, one by one, placing them all together—here, right now, on this island, fitting their lives together so they could finally heal.

She realized, now, part of her initial attraction to Ben was based on what had happened in that jungle village. Petras was her friend when she was a little girl. He made toys for her. Along with the other adults, he had watched out for her. She felt safe with Petras.

There had been something familiar about Ben from the moment she saw him striding up the hill after their fishing trip. And she was right. Those familiar broad shoulders, that unruly red hair, those stonemason hands had once, long ago, deliberately stood between her and death.

Just like she had felt safe with his father when she was a child, she felt safe with Ben now. She tried very hard not to think about the vacuum he would leave in her heart the day he left.

Chapter Twenty-Three

Ben found Moriah walking back and forth on the beach in front of the lighthouse.

"Something wrong?" he asked.

"Not really," Moriah said. "I'm just trying to gear myself up to tackle a carpentry job I don't want to do."

"What carpentry job?"

"Removing that built-in desk that's in the lighthouse keeper's office."

"The one you kept your sleeping bag and matches in?"

"That's the one."

"Why do you have to take it out?"

"The wall behind it is damaged. There's been a slow leak for years. I can't just patch around it. The desk will have to be removed and the wall repaired and painted. If I can keep from destroying it in the process I'll take the desk to a guy I know in Kagawong who will strip and refinish it. After that, I hope to re-install it."

"Sounds like a good plan." Ben skipped a rock across the water's surface. The lake had chosen to be as smooth as silk today. "So, what's the problem?"

"That wood is more than one hundred fifty years old. To take it out might damage it."

"Can you just crawl in and unscrew whatever is holding it to the wall?"

"Afraid not." She kicked a pebble into the water. "Screws were invented back then, but they weren't readily available. This desk is anchored with large, hand-wrought nails."

"You're saying you'll have to use a crowbar."

"I'll have to use a crowbar," Moriah said, "which could possibly split the wood and ruin the desk my great-great-grandfather made. I love that desk. If I destroy it, I'll never be able to live with myself."

Ben took her by the shoulders and gently turned her around to face him. "I know it has a lot of sentimental value to you, but it's just a desk. It doesn't feel anything. It's not alive. It doesn't have a soul. Liam Robertson made a nice desk. It was useful. People enjoyed it for decades. People will probably use it for decades more, but if you accidentally turn it into firewood, in the larger scheme of things, it really doesn't matter. Life gets so much simpler when you don't love things that can't love you back, lass."

"You're right." Moriah took a deep breath, let it out, and made herself relax. She stood looking at the lake for a moment longer and then smiled.

"Time to go get a crowbar. We'll see how this turns out."

An hour later, Ben was high up on some scaffolding. He glanced down and saw Moriah, Jack, and one of the other workers wrestling the oddly-shaped desk into her pickup. It appeared that it was still intact. Then Moriah and Jack climbed into the truck and sped off, presumably to take the desk to the refinisher. For Moriah's sake, he hoped it turned out well.

Chapter Twenty-Four

Moriah pulled her hair into a casual braid, donned her usual work boots, jeans, and t-shirt, and entered the lodge dining room with a light heart. They had made it into June with no mishaps, and the changes to the lighthouse tower were hard to miss. The top third of it had disappeared.

Ben expected to be finished taking down the tower by the end of June. The first part of July, they would pour a new concrete foundation. After the forms had been taken away and the concrete had cured, Lord willing, they would begin to lay the first course of stone.

Things were moving right along, and she was thrilled.

Even though she'd gotten up earlier than usual, Ben was already in the kitchen, a coffee cup at his elbow, his worn Bible and notebook in front of him.

It was interesting to her how much Ben had changed without really changing. The first time she'd laid eyes on him, she'd not thought he was particularly handsome. She had never liked red hair or freckles on a man. Now, when she came into the room, it struck her that he was one of the most gorgeous men she'd ever met. She had never realized how much getting to know another person's heart changed the way their outside appearance was perceived.

"Don't you ever get tired of the translating work you do?" She pulled out a chair and seated herself across the table from him.

"Actually, no." He thrust both arms up and stretched. "It's my cross-word puzzle, my chess game, my..."

Moriah held up a hand. "I get the picture. You enjoy your work."

"I enjoy my life, Moriah, especially now that you're in it. It's all play when your heart is joyful."

"Not if you're not a morning person, it isn't." Nicolas wandered into the dining room and plopped down beside of Ben. "I thought retirement would mean sleeping in."

"Didn't you sleep well?" Moriah went over to the kitchen counter, where the coffee pot gurgled, and poured a cup.

"No. I most emphatically did not."

Moriah held the pot out. "You want some?"

"Of course, I want some," Nicolas grouched. "Do you have an IV? If so, I shall inject the liquid directly into my veins."

Moriah sat a cup of steaming liquid in front of him. "What happened?"

"Your aunt came to my cabin in the middle of the night and asked me to go with her to help birth another baby on the reservation. Apparently, the word is out that an obstetrician is available at Kathy's beck and call. This is my third this month." He raised his voice so Katherine could hear him in the kitchen. "Why do these people insist on having so many babies during tourist season?"

"Long autumn nights, dear," Katherine called.

"Was the mother having a problem?" Moriah asked.

"No. She just had no way to get to the hospital. Probably not enough money, either. Everything went fine. In fact, after everything was over, while Kathy tended to the mother, I got to hold the baby."

"There's nothing sweeter than a newborn," Moriah said.

"I did enjoy it," Nicolas admitted. "I never got to hold them much when I was in private practice. The nurses always whisked the babies away to the pediatrician to be checked out." He traced a line down the white tablecloth with his finger, absorbed in his own thoughts. Then he glanced up and smiled. "Kathy promised to make biscuits as a reward for helping her last night."

"You're getting homemade biscuits for breakfast this morning?" Ben's voice was hopeful. "All I ate down at my cabin was cold cereal. I'm already hungry again." He raised his voice, "Hey, Katherine, wake me up next time you get a call for Nicolas. I bet I could figure out how to catch a baby. Let Nicolas sleep. I love babies, especially if homemade biscuits are involved."

Sometimes, Ben reminded Moriah of a big, cheerful, dog who regularly showed up at the lodge, hoping for a meal. Katherine rarely disappointed.

"And sausage gravy," Nicolas said.

"Wow." Ben sighed.

"I hear that," Katherine called. "And I've made enough for everyone, but it'll be a couple more minutes."

Nicolas peered at Ben's open Bible. "I forgot my glasses. How far have you gotten?"

"I'm starting into First Peter this morning. "

"You're making good progress, then."

"Yes, but I'm dreading Revelation. That's going to be a tough book to put into the Yahnowa language. I don't think they have a term for Great Dragon in Yahnowa."

"You might try using the term for Great Anaconda," Nicolas said. "They must have a word for that."

"They definitely have a word for that," Ben said.

Nicolas stifled a yawn. "I need a refill, I need my glasses…and I need a good-morning hug from Kathy." He wandered off into the kitchen.

Moriah grimaced.

"What?" Ben asked. "What's that face about? Don't you want your aunt getting a hug?"

"I just wish they weren't so…you know…so…"

"In love?"

"Well, so open about it."

"Think about it, Moriah. Neither of them dreamed they'd ever be together again, and now, they are. It's okay with me if they want to act like teenagers. Besides," he teased, "I think you're jealous. You want a good-morning hug, too." Ben pushed his chair back.

"I don't need hugs. I just…"

"Of course, you do." Ben stood, leaned across the table and gave her a bear hug that lifted her completely off her chair. Then he dropped her back into it.

"There, feel better?"

Moriah shook her head in mock dismay. "You are way, way too happy in the morning, Ben. "

"I'm living on a wonderful island, in a great cabin, spending time with a beautiful woman. What's not to like?"

Ben had called her beautiful again.

"In fact," Ben said. "I'm often surprised any of the men out at the work site can get any work done with you around."

"Yeah, right." Moriah made a face.

She knew Ben wasn't serious. In eighth grade she had shot up almost to her full height, towering over the other kids until some of them caught up in later grades. She had once overheard a boy call her "that big horsey girl" to some other kids. They had all laughed. It had hurt, of course. That was how she had thought of herself ever since, as a big horse of a girl.

Ben apparently saw her through different eyes, and she was happy about that, but she hadn't yet figured out how to gracefully react to Ben's compliments.

He closed his Bible, put his pens and papers in their case, and tucked everything beneath his arm.

"I need to gather a few things before we go to work." He headed out the door. "I'll be back in a few minutes."

As he left, she pictured the first day she had met him, how awkward he had been around her. That awkwardness hadn't lasted long. He was, at heart, a confident, intelligent, and talented man. He was a man who deserved to love and be loved by someone special. Someone who could go with him to the Amazon.

Chapter Twenty-Five

Moriah saw Chief Moawa's vicious, painted face behind every bush, behind every tree, behind every boulder. She was terrified and could not stop sobbing.

"Be quiet," Akawe demanded in a rough whisper. "If you want to live, stop crying!" She bit the inside of her mouth until it bled, swallowed her sobs, trembled with the effort to keep silent.

In spite of her valiant attempt to be quiet as Akawe and Rashawe maneuvered across a wet, creaking, rope bridge that spanned a deep gorge, a sudden cry escaped her lips. Akawe, startled, lost his balance. For an eternity, he fought, suspended over the gorge. Then, Rashawe thrust his spear toward him. Akawe caught it and regained his balance. Moriah, frozen with fear, immobilized and helpless, believed with all her heart that all three would plunge to their deaths if she ever again made the slightest sound.

With Katherine and Nicolas in the kitchen and Ben down at his cabin for a few minutes, Moriah poured herself a second cup of coffee and wandered over to the fireplace. She felt a little chilled, even though it was the dead of summer. The coldness, she knew, came entirely from within and the memories she now had to deal with almost on a daily basis.

Part of her wanted to shove them back inside the mental Pandora's

Box from which they'd emerged, but she knew she had to have the courage to face them if she was ever going to be whole. She sat down on one of the sofas, pulled an afghan around her shoulders, and closed her eyes.

The lift of the plane was frightening as it spirited her away. She felt small and helpless flying through the air with a stranger, a missionary priest from the convent school. He had been assigned to a new parish in Michigan and was packing for his trip when Akawe brought her to the school. Since the priest was already leaving, it was faster for Grandpa and Katherine to meet him at the airport in Detroit than for them to try to come to her. They were already on their way to Michigan, he told her.

The priest, a kind man, kept trying to cheer her up with little games and stories, but the knowledge that her mother and father were gone knotted her stomach into a giant, painful fist. She even shook her head at the snack the stewardess offered.

Her aunt and grandfather were waiting for her at the Detroit airport when she disembarked, and she clung to them, wordless, afraid to let go, afraid they'd disappear. They thanked the priest for accompanying her, and when her grandfather lifted her up in his arms, his face was wet with tears.

Katherine tried to comfort her as they drove home. "See Moriah? We're crossing the bridge back into Canada. We're getting closer and closer to home."

She buried her head in her aunt's lap as Grandpa drove and she chewed the ear off a stuffed bunny Katherine had brought along. She tried to ignore a roaring in her head that sounded like a giant waterfall as they crossed the long, rumbling bridge into Canada.

They traveled for hours into the heart of Ontario. Then, they waited in line to pull up onto a huge gangplank and into the bowels of the giant Chi-Cheemaun ferry. She heard the great clank of the motor and fought like a wild animal when Katherine tried to make her leave the car.

Katherine told her the other children ran about the ferry playing tag. Other children tossed bread crusts to seagulls circling the open deck. Other children begged nickels and dimes off their parents and ran to buy candy at the concession stand. It was fun on the ferry, Katherine said.

But Moriah refused. She wanted to stay in the car.

Staying in the car was not allowed by the ferry officials. They said it was dangerous. She fought like a tiger to stay. In the end, Katherine had to overpower her and carry her up the steep stairs of the ferry and into a large, open room. Moriah spent the rest of the two hour ferry ride in a fetal position ripping the other ear off the bunny with her baby teeth, while her aunt sat next to her, stroking her hair and crying.

After the ferry docked and they were allowed to get back into the car and drive off the ferry onto dry land, Katherine lifted Moriah to look out the window.

"We're on Manitoulin Island now, sweetie." She smoothed Moriah's hair away from her eyes. "You're safe here. Grandpa and I won't let anything bad happen to you. You won't ever have to go away to that bad place again. You're back on Manitoulin Island with us. You are in the safest place in the world."

Moriah jumped up from the sofa and pasted a smile on her face when Ben returned for breakfast. Nicolas and Katherine were carrying four plates heaped with food to the table.

"Katherine," Ben ogled the biscuits and gravy, "Will you marry me? We can have biscuits and gravy every morning? It will be a good life."

Nicolas sputtered and nearly dropped the plates. Moriah seated herself at the table, ignoring Ben's banter. She wasn't hungry. Not now. Not after reliving her trip from the jungle back to Manitoulin.

Katherine calmly sat the two plates she carried onto the table in front of Ben and Moriah. "Just say grace, Ben, and quit annoying Nicolas."

"Father, please keep us and our workers safe on the job today. Thank you for this food as well as for the gift of Katherine, who prepared it, and thank you for the fact that Moriah adores me. Amen." He slanted a glance in Moriah's direction.

"Just eat, Ben," she said. In spite of the melancholy she had felt moments before, she felt a little better. Ben's good nature had revived her, as usual.

"So, what are your plans today?" Nicolas shook out his napkin and centered it on his lap.

"Still working on bringing down the tower. It's tedious work. Plus, I suspect that the only thing holding some of it up was the metal stair structure inside." Ben poured a glass of juice from a pitcher sitting on the table. "We're having to disengage the inner staircase from the stones before we can bring them down. It isn't easy, but it can be done if we're careful."

"Will you be able to salvage the staircase?" Nicolas asked.

"I think so."

"I have an idea for the lighthouse, I would like to mention." Katherine said. Everyone stopped eating to stare. Katherine was the only one of them who'd not yet expressed an opinion about the restoration, even though she was the only one who had actually lived in the place. If she had an idea, they wanted to hear it.

"I think the appearance of the entire structure would benefit by laying a stone wall around it, cottage included." Katherine's voice was slightly apologetic. "I know it would be a lot of work, but my mother saw a picture of a lighthouse once that had a low stone wall surrounding it. A flower garden had been planted within, and my mother always wanted to do the same. She and Dad had to move out before they could get around to it."

Everyone was silent, contemplating the image.

Nicolas made a decision. "I'll pay extra."

"What do you think?" Moriah asked Ben.

"She's right. I should have thought of it earlier. It's exactly what the place needs. A dry stone wall, one without mortar, would be best. It could shift with the extremes of temperature that you get on this island. There is much loose stone lying around, and it would be a good way to use some of it."

"Could you teach me?" Moriah said. "I'd like to learn how to build a stone wall."

"Of course," Ben said, "I'll give you a lesson today if you want."

Chapter Twenty-Six

"Okay," Moriah said as soon as they'd given assignments to the other workers. "How do I start?"

"You start by gathering lots of stones," Ben said.

"Then what?"

"Then you get lots and lots more stones."

"Okay already. I heard you. Then what?"

"Then you get more stones."

Moriah put her hands on her hips, tilted her head to one side, and lifted an eyebrow. "Stop it."

"I'm serious. A job this big is going to require days of rock gathering. Before I can teach you a thing, we have to gather a big pile of stones."

With a sigh, Moriah pulled on a pair of gloves and bent to lift a large stone lying at her feet.

As she lifted it, something moved beneath, and she jumped back so quickly, she stumbled and fell backwards. A snake slithered out of a small crevice beneath the rock and wound its way quickly down the hill toward the lake.

"Are you okay?" Ben helped her up.

"It wasn't poisonous." She nervously rubbed her hands up and down her arms. "If it isn't a Massasauga, and it's on Manitoulin, it's not poisonous. That's what Black Hawk said."

"Very good. Does that mean you aren't afraid of them anymore?"

"Not quite as much as I was."

"Good girl." He patted her on top of her head.

She batted his hand away. "Aren't you afraid of them?"

"No, I'm not. I avoid them, but I can't allow myself to fear them, or I'd never be able to build. Snakes enjoy hiding around stone, so they kind of come with the job. The only thing worse than snakes is a wasp or hornet nest. Now *those* are fun to stick your hand into."

"That's happened to you?"

"Oh yeah. More than once." Ben grimaced.

"I don't know what a stonemason gets paid, Ben, but whatever it is, it isn't enough."

"And I think that is something you need to tell Nicolas," he said, solemnly. "Now, about these rocks you'll be helping me gather…"

He hefted the one she had dropped. "Building a wall is a whole lot like working a jigsaw puzzle, except it's a lot better than a puzzle because, when you finish, you will have created something that can stand for generations."

He squatted, picked up another rock from the dozens dotting the immediate area, and then experimentally fitted them against the one she had selected.

"Every stone is different. They all have their own unique personalities. That's what makes rock walls so much more interesting and pleasing to the eye than standardized concrete blocks. The eye naturally enjoys variety."

He selected another stone and placed it beside the others. "There are always a few stones that don't seem to fit anywhere. You keep trying to fit them in, and you keep trying, but they don't work. Then, all at once, you'll find a hole that seems like it was made for that odd-shaped rock you were ready to toss."

He placed a fourth stone. "A rock wall always reminds me of a church. There's always someone who doesn't seem to fit. Then, one day, that person finds the right niche, the right ministry, and the church community is stronger for them being there."

Moriah knelt beside him, watching his hands, listening intently.

"When the hard winters and the hot summers come, the wall can expand and contract and remain intact longer for the very reason that each stone is different from the others. It's a nice thing to remember when you fall into thinking the world would be a better place if everyone was exactly the same as you."

He placed another stone beside the others. "Bet you didn't expect a sermon *and* a lesson on building walls."

"Is that the kind of stuff you think about when you build?" Moriah asked.

"Sometimes. Laying a dry stone wall takes patience and persistence. It gives a person plenty of time to think."

Ben stood and stretched his back. "Now, you try your hand at this while I gather more stones."

Chapter Twenty-Seven

Moriah worked on the stone wall all day with Ben's encouragement and supervision. If it began to veer a bit to one side or another, he always found just the right rock to make up the difference.

"You're doing great," Ben said. "This isn't easy to learn. Most people give up, but you're doing it. I'm proud of you."

She was discovering that her back had muscles she'd never known existed, and all of them ached, but Ben was so pleased with the job she was doing, she was determined to keep going.

Instead of working on the tower, he left Jack in charge and spent the day gathering stones from all around the peninsula. She was amazed to find there were so many different colors, shapes, and sizes. She had never really noticed the variety before.

Occasionally, he had to place a large one, a rock bigger than she could lift, in the wall to work the smaller ones around. It gave the wall strength and character, he said, and then he pointed out that it was like when God made people with greater gifts to help hold the church together.

Moriah had never given any thought to her place in her church—her part in holding up the "wall." As she fitted the rocks together, she realized that, in her obsession to make and save enough money to purchase the lighthouse, she had allowed herself to become a rather small pebble at her church.

Ben was right. Building a stone wall gave a person plenty of time to think. Maybe too much.

Petras was carrying rocks from the river near their village, preparing to build a room onto the clinic. She was not allowed to go to the river, but he was a grownup man, so he could go wherever he wanted. Seeing him go back and forth from the river to the clinic, carrying dripping rocks, was fascinating. She crept closer and closer. Before long, she had followed Petras almost the whole way.

"You are a curious little lass, aren't you," he said. "I'd better get you back to your mother." He dropped the rock he had pulled from the river onto the path and picked her up. He placed her on his shoulders and walked back toward the village.

She had never ridden on Petras' shoulders before. He was bigger than Daddy, and she liked being up so high. She did not like it when he stopped in the middle of the path and stood completely still.

"Go!" she urged.

Petras told her to shush and pointed up the path several yards.

At first, she didn't see it, and then she did. A giant snake was slithering across the path. It was very big, and it took a long time for it to cross. Petras waited and waited, standing very still, even long after it had disappeared.

"What was that?" she asked.

"It was an Anaconda," Petras said.

"What's an Anaconda?"

"A very large snake." He started walking again.

"Does it bite?"

"No," he said. "It swallows things whole."

"Does it eat little girls?"

"Sometimes," he said, "especially little girls who disobey their mother and go to the river when they have been told not to."

He gave her back to her mother with a warning about the big snake.

Her mother did not have to chastise her. Moriah was too frightened ever to go to the river again. She didn't want to get swallowed by a big snake.

At the end of the day, with Ben's occasional help, she had completed a course of stone wall ten feet long and three feet high. In spite of having worn work gloves, her fingers were bruised and scraped in several places. She stood back and admired her work with as much pride as she had taken in the first cabin she had ever built.

"It usually takes a lot longer than this to teach someone how to lay stone," Ben said. "You're quick."

"It doesn't seem like I got all that far."

"It's not how far you get in one day; it's how well you build, how strong. A wall like that will stand a hundred years and beyond with only minor repairs from time to time. You did well."

"Thanks." She drew off her gloves and stuffed them into her back pocket. "Let's go see how much the guys have gotten done inside the cottage today. Are we on track for the light tower?"

"Two more weeks and I should be able to start rebuilding your precious light tower." Ben tugged her braid. "You are as bad as a kid at Christmas."

Chapter Twenty-Eight

"You've added, what? Another five feet?" Ben said, when he came at lunchtime to check on her. "Good job!"

She stood up, wiped her face with her forearm, and took a step back to admire what she had done. "Feels like it should be a mile, as hard as it has been."

"But you're enjoying it."

"I am."

"Katherine will be very pleased."

"She should be." Moriah stretched her back. "Every bone in my body aches. I think I'm going to have as much muscle as you by the time I get this wall finished."

"That's okay," Ben said. "I'll still love you."

Moriah's stomach flipped over. Had he actually meant to say that he loved her? Or was it just a phrase he had used, something he'd tossed out without thinking?

Ben seemed not to realize the impact his words had on her. He was already talking about something else. She missed everything, except the last two words.

"...more stones." He looked at her expectantly, waiting for her reply.

"Excuse me?" she said.

"I said you've almost run out of stones. Your pile is nearly gone." He pointed down to the lake, where a tumble-down stone boat house squatted at the edge. "I was asking if you thought it would be a good idea to bring those rocks up here and incorporate them into the wall. The boat house isn't really usable anymore."

"Sure," she said. "I'll get right on it."

"No need," he said. "You keep working here. I'll take the truck down and select the best ones. It won't take long. I'll get Jack to help me."

"Sounds great, thanks."

Moriah was so intent on what she was doing that she didn't pay any attention to what was going on at the old boat house. In fact, she had rarely ever paid any attention to it. At one time, it had been used to house a small life boat in case the keeper needed to go rescue people from a ship wreck. After the lighthouse was decommissioned, the life boat got stolen, and vines took over the small stone structure. Taking it apart would remove an eyesore.

She felt a touch on her shoulder and turned around. It was Jack, and he had a strange look on his face.

"Moriah, I think you need to come with me." His voice was gentle.

"What's wrong?"

"Ben…"

"Ben!" She whirled around to look at the old boat house. "Has he been hurt?"

"No. He's fine. He just said you need to come down there."

"Why?"

"He's found something in the boat house we think you need to see."

Moriah ran down the hill to where Ben was. It looked like he and Jack had already moved the old boards that had once been part of a low roof. Quite a lot of stone from it had been moved to the truck. She saw that Ben was kneeling on the ground inside the boat house looking at something on the ground.

"What's wrong?" she said, when she reached him.

He stood up, and she noticed that he had a dry paint brush in his hand. She could think of no reason he would need a paint brush down here.

"I'm sorry, but I think you need to see this, Moriah."

She looked at the place where he had been kneeling. Suddenly, she saw why he was holding the brush. She gasped and threw her hand over her mouth.

He bent over and flicked a bit more dirt away from a human skeleton.

"What on earth!" she said. "Who?"

"I have no idea," Ben said. "But I'm pretty sure they've been here a very long time."

Chapter Twenty-Nine

"How did you find this?" Moriah asked.

"When we got the vines cleared away a bit, I saw there were some large, flat stones that formed the floor. I thought they might be useful to make a bit of a patio outside the back door of the cottage, but when I pulled them up, there were ashes beneath."

"Ashes?"

"We thought that was odd, but we went ahead and moved all the floor stones, anyway. While we were scuffling around, carrying them out of here, we noticed that there were bones beneath the ashes. It's a very shallow grave. That's when Jack got me a clean paint brush and I started brushing the dirt and ash away from it."

"How are things going?" Katherine called.

Nicolas was walking behind her, carrying a large basket. "We brought a picnic. Katherine thought it might be nice to come out, see how things are progressing, and relax a bit...what are you three looking at?"

"The question isn't what we're looking at, it is *who* we are looking at," Ben said. "Apparently, someone buried a body here."

"Seriously?" Nicolas handed the basket to Katherine. "Let me take a look."

Ben, Jack, and Moriah stood aside so the doctor could see what they had discovered.

Nicolas crouched beside the skeleton and brushed away more dirt, revealing that the person had been buried in a heavy, ragged, woolen coat. The pants, which were thinner, had rotted away, revealing long underwear laced with holes. He also wore disintegrating leather boots.

Nicolas stood up. "Male, about 6 feet tall. Looks like maybe size twelve shoes."

Bending over, he brushed away more dirt from what would have been the face. As the dirt fell away from the skull, it was possible to see the teeth. A glint of gold captured their attention.

"Is that a gold tooth?" Katherine asked.

Nicolas flicked away more loose dirt. "It certainly is."

"Liam Robertson had a gold tooth," Katherine said.

"Your great-grandfather?" Nicolas asked. "The one who went missing?"

"Yes. My grandfather told me that *his* father, Zachary Robertson, had once mentioned that his father, Liam, had a gold tooth. It was rare to have one in these parts back then. He got it somewhere overseas while serving in the Navy."

"The state of the skeleton and clothing could be from that far back," Nicolas said.

"That's what I thought," Ben said.

"Look at this." Nicolas picked up the skull and turned it so everyone could see a large, ragged, hole in the back of it. "I know I'm an obstetrician with no forensic training, but if this is Liam Robertson, I think there's a strong chance that he didn't just disappear into the woods. This looks like blunt head trauma."

"I'm going to go call the police," Moriah said. "Even if the body is over a hundred years old. I don't know what else to do."

"I believe I've just lost my appetite for ham sandwiches," Katherine said. "I'll go with you."

"Why the ashes, I wonder," Ben said, after Moriah and Katherine left to go back to the lodge to make a phone call.

"You've never spent a winter this far north, have you?" Nicolas said.

"No, I haven't."

"Then you don't know that a death in the middle of winter causes all sorts of complications, even today," Nicolas said. "Back then, many families had to keep their deceased frozen in a shed until spring, when the ground warmed up enough to dig a proper grave. Sometimes, if for some reason they were truly desperate to bury a body, they would create a huge bonfire and keep it going to help things along by thawing out the ground beneath. In the middle of the winter, when Liam was supposed to have disappeared, it would have taken a large bonfire to make it possible to dig even a shallow grave. Instead of six feet, this one is what, maybe a foot deep? It was probably all they could manage during a hard winter. Even today, the undertaker has to keep the body of the deceased in cold storage until the ground thaws enough to dig a grave."

"But do you really think it might have been murder?" Ben said.

"I don't have enough training in that area to know for sure," Nicolas said. "But if it was an accident, like a bad fall, then who buried him? Only his wife and son were with him. Who else would be around to do that in the middle of winter? And why would Eliza Robertson tell the authorities that her husband had disappeared if she already knew he had died from some sort of accident?"

"Do you suppose someone else might have killed and buried him without her knowing?"

"I don't think she could have missed seeing a giant bonfire." Nicolas said.

"So, you think Eliza might have killed her husband, buried the body, and pretended that he disappeared?" Jack asked.

"If this is Liam, it's possible." Nicolas said. "The story I remember

Kathy's father telling me was that Liam and Eliza had been cooped up all winter, alone with their child. The nearest thing to civilization was something like eleven miles away. Cabin fever can do strange things to human minds. People under those kinds of circumstances have been killed for not much more than looking at someone the wrong way."

It took the Manitoulin policeman about twenty minutes to get there. Word spread fast, and the crew soon put down their tools and came to see what was going on. Some of the older people, who loved to watch the progress on the lighthouse, also came to take a look.

"Murder or not, there's not a whole lot we can do about it now," the young policeman said.

"I have a friend who teaches forensics in Toronto," Nicolas said. "Can you help make arrangements to have what's left of the body taken to him?"

"We can do that." The officer nodded, pleased to have a direction. Murder was rare on Manitoulin, but he knew the protocol just in case. He hadn't been sure what to do in a case like this and was happy to follow Nicolas's suggestion.

Chapter Thirty

The stones from the boathouse were removed, the flat ones incorporated into a back patio that he built with them. The other boathouse stones were used in the wall Moriah had just finished with a good bit of help from Ben. There was nothing left to indicate there had ever been a boathouse or a shallow grave, which was just as well.

"You're finished with the wall?" Nicolas walked over from the lodge, while she and Ben were admiring their handiwork. "Kathy's going to love this."

"I hope so," Moriah said.

"I came over to tell you that I got a call back from my friend in Toronto, the forensic expert," Nicolas said. "I thought you might want to hear his report."

"Definitely," Moriah said.

"His findings match the time period when Liam Robertson would have lived. We didn't search his clothing, but my friend did. An inside pocket held a cheap pocket watch with Liam's name engraved on the back. I don't think there is any doubt that the skeleton was of your great, great grandfather, Moriah."

"So, could your expert tell for sure how he died?"

"It looks like I was right in my original assumption. It was the head injury as far as he could tell. No one comes to my mind as a suspect except Eliza."

"How very strange to think that Eliza might have done something like that," Moriah said. "She's always been a heroine of mine, taking over the duties of a light keeper after her husband disappeared. Raising her son out here alone."

"Sometimes even decent women are driven to do bad things," Nicolas said. "If she killed him, apparently, she lived a virtuous life from that moment on. There was never any suspicion about her when I was growing up here. It would be interesting to know what drove her to it, assuming she did."

"About all we have are assumptions," Moriah said. "I wish there was a way to know for sure. I wish we had the logbook."

"I doubt the logbook would say anything along the lines of, 'Oh, and by the way, I killed my husband today,'" Ben said.

"True," Moriah said. "Well, regardless of what happened, I want to give him a proper burial when we get his remains back."

"I agree," Nicolas said. "He was your blood kin, one of the first light keepers on this island, and he deserves to have a dignified burial."

Chapter Thirty-One

It was a beautiful evening in July as Moriah built a fire on the sandy beach. They and their crew had accomplished a staggering amount of work. Of course, there was still much more to do. The temperature was balmy. A small breeze blew in gently off the lake, just enough to make the bit of warmth from a bonfire feel welcome. A full moon cast light on the water. Most guests stayed from Sunday afternoon to Saturday morning, so the Friday night bonfire on the beach had become a tradition to wrap up the week.

There was usually a general camaraderie that developed between guests over the space of a vacation week at the resort. Friday night, before they went home, tended to become a time of reflection, soaking up the last moments of unhurried vacation, enjoying the wild sound of a loon, once more, as it wafted over the lake from their secret places. There were lazy discussions about large fish either caught or lost. Some of the guests brought folding lawn chairs. Some preferred to relax on blankets on the beach. It was Moriah's favorite time of the week.

This had been an especially good week for her. Everything had worked properly in the cabins, all the toilets flushed, everyone got along, and no one fell overboard during their fishing excursions. Nicolas had become quite the inn keeper as he helped Katherine. Baby Betsy had charmed guests as Alicia lent a hand each day. The baby had taken her first steps only yesterday. Having Alison and Nicolas there meant

Katherine could get in a few days at her part-time job at Wikwemikong.

In other words, it was working.

She took mental stock of all they had accomplished. The slate roof on the cottage had been removed and new trusses set up. Then, a new roof was installed using as many of the old slates as possible. Once that was in place, the work on the inside had begun. The basics of plumbing and furnace installation took up some of the time. A sewage system was put in, insulated windows installed. The limestone of the cottage was power-washed of decades of grime. The inside was still unfinished, but from the outside, the cottage shone.

In the midst of all this organized chaos, they buried Liam Robertson's remains in the small family cemetery that had been filling up with Robertson relatives for over a century. With Ben officiating, they laid one of the area's first light keepers to rest in the ground with a proper service. Ben created a headstone out of one of the hand-hewn pieces of broken limestone they were replacing on the light tower.

"It's beautiful," Moriah said, when she saw the image he'd carved. "Thank you."

It was an image of their light house with waves crashing about it, above Liam Robertson's name, date of birth, and approximate date of death.

"I don't get to indulge often," he said. "But I do enjoy a bit of fancy work every now and then."

Except for a few scrapes, bruises, and a couple strained back and shoulder muscles, none of their crew had suffered any harm. No rain was expected for several days, so the foundation had been poured today. They would let the concrete cure over the weekend; come Monday, the process of rebuilding the tower would begin. The weather was supposed to be fine for several days so the timing was working out perfectly.

She could hardly wait to see it rise, strong and new. Ben was right.

She was as excited as a kid at Christmas.

As the resort guests began to gather, Moriah sat back in the shadows, contentedly watching and savoring their enjoyment.

There was a lot to complain about in running a place like this, but there were many blessings, too. Tonight, it felt as though the blessings far outweighed the complaints.

It pleased her that one of the guests had brought his guitar to the Friday night gathering. He and his wife made their living as musicians, and they were very good. The wife had brought her violin with her. They tuned up, and soon, a sweet folk melody began to fill the soft summer air.

Work finished for the day, Nicolas and Katherine sat with their backs against a log, holding hands, relaxing with their guests. Moriah watched the firelight flicker over her aunt's face and saw true joy there. They had set their wedding day for the end of August. It would be very simple. There was little time to do anything too elaborate, but Katherine would have her church wedding, and Moriah would be the maid of honor. She had never seen her aunt so happy. She closed her eyes and allowed the music and the feeling of contentment to flow over her.

She opened them again, when she caught the scent of Ben's shaving soap, and felt his body settling down next to hers on the sand.

"Nice fire," he said. "What a lovely night!"

She nodded. "All of it. The wind, the lake, the sand, the music, the full moon. It's pretty close to perfect."

They were such good friends, so comfortable with each another. Aside from Ben's teasing compliments, they had managed to make it through much of the summer without embarrassing themselves by openly acknowledging the attraction they felt toward one another.

But right at this moment, with the music and the moonlight and the soft breeze from the lake, plus the intimacy of sitting somewhat apart from the rest of the group, with Ben's shoulder just touching hers, she couldn't help wishing they could be more than friends.

Apparently, Ben felt the same way. With no warning, he pushed her hair back behind her ear, leaned in, and kissed it.

"Ben!" She was shocked and delighted. "Someone will see!"

"I doubt anyone would be surprised."

"But, Ben…"

"I know what you're going to say. We have issues. I agree. I can't stay, and you can't go. But, I've wanted to do that for such a long time."

Her skin still tingled from the touch of his lips. "Since when?"

"Since I saw you lying on the couch after I carried you to the lodge. Katherine was in the kitchen getting a wet cloth for your forehead, and you were still unconscious. I took the liberty of brushing your hair back out of your eyes and tucking it behind your ear. It struck me then that you had the velvetiest skin, the silkiest hair, and the longest lashes I had ever seen. I had never met anyone I thought more perfect."

"I'm far from perfect," she said. "You know that."

"I think the eye of the beholder gets to decide that."

His gaze upon her was so intense that she had to look away. Two more seconds of looking into his blue eyes, and she would fling herself at him and beg him to marry her.

She couldn't let that happen, even though her heart was breaking from the effort of holding back. Unless she could overcome her cursed weakness about leaving this island, she was going to lose him. She turned her head, so he wouldn't see the tears that were beginning to fill her eyes.

"I stepped over a boundary that I shouldn't have," he said. "I apologize, lass. It was the music and the night. Let's just enjoy this beautiful evening together, without trying to figure anything out."

Chapter Thirty-Two

As the light tower grew and the keeper's cottage neared completion, the preparations for the wedding escalated.

Then, suddenly, the wedding day arrived, and everyone was scurrying around, either helping or getting in the way. Moriah had given the crew the day off in celebration and a chance to come to the wedding if they wanted.

The phone was ringing as Ben entered the lodge, but no one answered. He heard the shower running upstairs, probably Moriah getting an early start on preparing for her big day as Katherine's maid of honor.

The tourist season was finally winding down as families went home to get children ready for school, but several of the remaining guests were pitching in to help with the wedding. Today, all of Katherine and Nicolas's plans and preparations would come together.

Since no one seemed interested in the fact that the phone was ringing, he answered it.

"Robertson's Resort. Can I help you?"

"Ben?" The voice sounded far away.

"Yes."

"It's me. Abraham."

Ben's heart lurched. Abraham and his wife, Violet, were the two elderly missionaries helping him with the Yahnowa tribe. If Abraham was calling, something was terribly wrong. It was a hard, two-day trek from their village to the nearest telephone.

"What's wrong, brother?" Ben gripped the phone tightly against his ear.

"It's Violet. She's sick."

"How sick?"

"She doesn't want me to tell you about it."

"Why?"

"She's modest."

"I know she's modest, but what's wrong?" Ben's chest was pounding. He had hated to leave those two alone. Abraham was a hale seventy-year-old, but Violet was frail. She compensated by possessing a lion's heart and an enormous love for the Yahnowa people, but still…

"She thinks she might have bowel cancer, Ben."

"How long has she suspected?"

"Since before you left."

"And she didn't tell anyone?"

"She hoped the problem would go away. Even I didn't know."

"Where is she now?"

"Back at the village. She feels too bad to trek out. I'm arranging for a helicopter, but she's worried about leaving our people. She thinks there will be trouble if one of us isn't there."

"Why?"

"There's been some revenge killings by two tribes near us in the south. There's been talk. She's afraid it will spread to the Yahnowa. You know how that kind of thing can spill over."

"Yes. I know." Ben pondered the situation. Amazon tribes frequently made the feud between the Hatfield's and McCoy's look like a tea party. Entire tribes had been wiped out before the arrival of the missionaries and after.

"I'm sorry to ask this, Ben, but we need you to come back as soon as possible. Aren't you nearly done there?"

Ben made some quick calculations. He had intended to finish mortaring the top run of stone on the tower by noon, just in time to get ready to be Nicolas's best man.

The shower shut off above him, and he stared at the ceiling. He hated the idea of breaking the news of an early, unexpected departure to Moriah

"Ben?" Abraham's voice was uncharacteristically querulous. "Ebenezer? Are you there?"

He had no choice. He had an obligation greater his desire to spend more time with Moriah.

"I'll leave tomorrow morning," Ben said.

"You need to plan to stay awhile, Ben," Abraham said. "Even if Violet doesn't have cancer, I don't think we'll be coming back. I've been having a few dizzy spells, myself. I'm afraid we're done. We'll try to find someone to come take our place, but it might take some time."

"I understand. I'll take care of things." Ben's mind began to calculate logistics.

One day. He only had one day left with Moriah, and it was already filled with a wedding.

"Thank you," Abraham said. "I knew you would come."

"Give Violet my love. Tell her I'm praying for her."

Ben hung up. He grabbed the phone book, dialed, and scheduled his flight. Leaving Manitoulin Island...and Moriah...was going to be the hardest thing he had ever done, but he no longer had a choice.

Chapter Thirty-Three

Ben mortared the last stone into place and completed his portion of the light house. There was still the lantern room to build on top of the tower, with metal bracings and new oak beams. It would take Moriah awhile longer without him, but she had a good crew; she could do it.

Working from old photographs that Katherine had unearthed, Moriah planned to duplicate that lantern room exactly with the exception of the Fresnel lens. His task had only been to make the tower strong again—and that he had done.

Moriah had worked wonders on the keeper's cottage. It still needed a bit more attention, but it was looking good. Katherine had come to the work site with the bed of the resort truck filled with nursery annuals. She had planted flowers all along the stone wall. It was already looking spectacular.

He had gone to see Sam Black Hawk, hoping for information about the Fresnel lens, but he didn't tell Moriah he believed it might have survived the vandalism. There was no reason to get her hopes up, unless it was actually in his possession. The visit had been a disappointment. Black Hawk pretended to have no knowledge of the lens and denied he had ever mentioned it.

Ben and Moriah had already planned the celebration party for the completion of the lighthouse. They intended to invite everyone from the community. He had planned to rig some sort of illumination in the

tower, creating a grand finale—the light glimmering on the lake again after so many years of darkness.

Now, he was going to miss it.

But that wasn't all he was going to miss. He had been holding off until the tower was completed to propose to Moriah. Even though they had not yet expressed it, he knew she was in love with him, and he loved her. He had visualized the moment for weeks, intending to ask her to marry him while they were standing high atop this massive work that they had both poured their hearts into. To him, it was symbolical, a sign that, with God's help, they could conquer anything—even her inability to leave the island. Somehow, someway, he knew they could find a way to be together without breaking his promise to the Yahnowa and to God.

He struggled with himself. To ask her now would mean to abandon her tomorrow morning. To *not* ask her now, to leave with nothing but a hug might mean losing her altogether.

Ben wiped his hands on a rag and climbed down the scaffolding. Tomorrow, his crew would begin attaching the original iron spiral staircase to the inside of the light tower. The staircase would wind its way up the eighty feet of limestone he had just finished setting.

He wished he could be there to see it all come together.

Moriah would be able to finish the rest of the work without him. He was certain of that. His only concern was leaving her with an all-male crew to supervise. Jack would watch out for her, he reassured himself. No one would dare try anything with that blonde giant about.

Ben smiled at the image. Jack was big enough to put the fear of God into any man who might be bold enough to lay a finger on Moriah. Of course, Moriah was fully capable of braining a man with a shovel if he tried anything with her, as well. It was one of her many charms.

He dropped off the bottom rung, put his tools away, and climbed into the truck. Nicolas and Katherine's wedding would take place in two hours. It was the only reason Moriah wasn't here beside him. Because of the wedding, she had made an unprecedented appointment at Brenda's Barbering and Hairdressing. He couldn't wait to see her in the maid-of-honor finery that Katherine had bought for her in the mall at Espanola.

If he asked her to marry him, would she follow him later to Brazil? Could she?

He knew she had made a couple trips alone to the bridge this summer that she hadn't told him about. Nicolas had seen her one night pacing the ground in front of it. He said she had stood for the longest time, staring at the bridge. Finally, she had turned around and came back home without crossing. Sam mentioned that he had heard from others who had seen her haunting the bridge as well.

Ben was certain she was trying to overcome this problem all by herself, and he wasn't happy about it. In fact, it hurt a little. He would go with her. He would hold her hand while she crossed, or carry her over on his back if she wanted.

He had hoped her fear would go away, once her memory had returned, but she avoided the subject each time he tried to bring it up. He had done the only thing he knew—prayed until he hoped God would become so tired of his entreaties that He would answer Ben's prayer just to shut him up. He didn't have the knowledge or the skill to make Moriah well. God did.

He glanced at the rearview mirror. The tower stood tall and straight behind him. Stone upon stone. Word upon word. That's what he knew how to do. The inner workings of Moriah's mind remained a mystery to him.

Covered in mortar and rock dust, he entered his cabin and emerged forty-five minutes later in a black tuxedo, white shirt, and an emerald vest and tie.

The whole wedding had become a much bigger deal than Ben had expected. Even though she'd kept the decorations relatively simply, Katherine had expanded her plans to a wedding with what seemed to be half the island in attendance. The church would be filled to capacity this afternoon.

When he arrived at the lodge, caterers from the mainland were putting the finishing touches on a feast. He hoped there might be some spare bite of food lying about as he wandered into the dining room.

"Hello, Ben. "

He gulped. One glance at Moriah, and he forgot all about being hungry. She looked incredible. Her hair was pulled up into a cascade of glistening black curls, tendrils spiraling down around her face. Her eyes and mouth had just the right amount of makeup. Her dress was an off-the-shoulder emerald green that exactly matched her eyes.

She smiled at his reaction, the whiteness of her teeth enhanced by her tawny skin and the deep shade of burgundy on her lips. Luscious lips. He had never thought of anyone's lips as luscious, but it was exactly the right adjective for Moriah's.

Was this truly the same woman who had worked beside him all summer?

She had lost a little weight—not that she had needed to, of course—but her dress showed off a perfect waist and shoulders. It draped about her, flaring slightly at the bottom. She made a little gesture and held it out.

"I feel like a trussed-up turkey, Ben."

"You look like an angel. No, that isn't right. You look like an Irish fairy princess. That's better." He was nearly stuttering in his appreciation. There simply weren't words to describe his Moriah. "You look like a mermaid. You're…"

"Stunning," Nicolas supplied the word Ben had been searching for, "as is her aunt."

Katherine practically floated down the staircase. She had opted for an ankle-length ivory gown of lace with a high collar. The dress reminded Ben of a much earlier time. He was no expert on women's dresses, but he had heard this kind of style referred to as Victorian. Her hair hung loose, a dark cloud of soft curls with tiny, white flowers tucked here and there. He had never seen Katherine without her hair scrapped back into tight braids. For the first time, he could see a glimpse of the girl with whom Nicolas had once fallen in love.

Brenda-the-hairdresser must be really, really good, Ben decided, or maybe, it wasn't entirely the beautician's magic; maybe it was love that was giving Katherine that glow. He could only imagine what it must have cost Nicolas to give her up when they were young. With all his heart, he silently congratulated them on the new life they were starting together.

"Is the groom supposed to see the bride before the wedding?" he asked. "I thought I heard somewhere that's bad luck."

"I don't believe in luck," Nicolas said, "and there's no good place at the church for our girls to change into their finery. So, Ben, are you ready to help me escort them?"

Ben's reply was heartfelt. "Anytime, anywhere."

Chapter Thirty-Four

Moriah held her bouquet in her lap and sat very still, trying not to disturb her hairdo, as she sat in the backseat of Nicolas's black Mercedes. She had decided, while her head was being lathered over a bowl, that if she was smart enough to build a cabin, repair a lighthouse, and build a stone wall, she was probably smart enough to figure out this girlie stuff, and she wanted to. It was worth the time and cost to see that look of awe on Ben's face. And it was much nicer than chopping her own hair off every six months with Katherine's sewing scissors.

While traveling to the church, she surreptitiously admired her fingernails. Long, lovely nails, and they were all hers. She had paid good money for them. Her fingers had never looked so graceful.

Ben glanced down, focused on her hands, and she eagerly anticipated his reaction. Nothing there to be ashamed of today. No ragged cuticles, no broken nails, just a smooth, unbroken, satiny burgundy nail polish.

"What in the world?" Ben peered at her hands. "What did you do?"

"I had my nails done."

"Why? They were fine before."

"Oh, Ben. I didn't want to look like a man today."

"Lass," Ben's voice was strained, "with that body and that face, you couldn't look like a man if you tried."

Moriah smiled. Yes, the trouble she and the women at the beauty shop had gone to was worth it.

"You're hands look pretty, sweetheart." He took one of her hands in his and studied her fingernails. "But then, they always do to me."

He lifted her hand to his lips, gazing at her with those deep blue eyes of his, and kissed it.

It took her breath away.

He had also taken her breath away when she first glimpsed him as he strolled into the lodge wearing that tux. His latest haircut had grown out, curling slightly over the stiff, white collar. His blue eyes were startling against the tan he had gradually obtained in spite of the sunscreen.

He did not release her hand but continued to hold it as they drove to the church.

She was grateful they had another month ahead of them while they completed the project. There was unspoken hope in her heart that he would decide to stay. There were good signs. He never complained about being on the island, and he was making a lot of friends among the people at church and the crew. She knew he admired and cared about her.

She would never ask him to stay here to be with her, but if he decided on his own to live permanently on the island, instead of going back to live in the Amazon, she would not fight him about it.

If they were to be together, he would have to stay.

She had secretly tried to leave the island this summer. Over and over. In the middle of the night, while everyone else was asleep and she knew the swing bridge wouldn't be moving to accommodate ships.

She had tried driving across it; she had tried walking across it. Nothing had worked. She told no one, not even Ben. This was her fight, her struggle. The failure she felt each time her fear defeated her was not something she wished to share with anyone.

Her attempts had felt like death each time. The dizziness, the chest pain, the shaking, and the dry mouth. The same feelings that had terrified her as a child washed over her each time she tried.

Except now, she had the desperation of her love for Ben and the horrific flashbacks to her childhood in the Amazon to add to her private bag of misery.

Ben was worth it, she told herself each time she arose in the middle of the night to drive to Little Current to attack the bridge again.

Ben was worth everything.

Chapter Thirty-Five

The church was filled with friends, while Katherine and Nicolas made their vows to each other. Nicolas had a surprisingly hard time getting through the service without crying. Katherine was serene and happy.

Ben and Moriah gazed into one another's eyes, while standing beside the bride and groom as vows were said. Moriah fantasized about repeating the same words to Ben someday.

The wedding was beautiful, and the reception came off without a hitch. Then, after the reception, Nicolas and Katherine drove away in a flurry of good wishes. Katherine blew the crowd a kiss as they turned onto the highway. There was a collective sigh from the crowd as the newlyweds disappeared from sight, bound for a well-deserved honeymoon.

The caterers made quick work of cleaning up the debris. The guests went home, and the few tourists who were still staying at the resort, drifted back to their cabins. Moriah found herself alone in the lodge with Ben, both still dressed in their wedding finery.

"It was a nice wedding," Moriah said. "I didn't expect Nicolas to be so emotional."

"I had a pretty big lump in my throat, as well." Ben captured one of her hands and drew her down onto the couch beside him. "All I could think about was how much I wished it was us saying our vows."

She hesitated a moment and then said, "I was thinking the same thing."

There. It was said. The feelings they had for each other were out in the open. Now what?

Moriah's heart beat so hard she wondered if he could hear it. "But I still can't leave the island."

She waited for him to tell her that if she truly couldn't leave the island, he would stay. Instead, his brow furrowed, and he looked pained and worried.

"Are you sure, Moriah? A lot of things have happened since the summer began. You are a stronger person now than you were."

"I've tried to cross the bridge several times since you came, Ben, but I can't. I just can't do it. I'm so sorry, Ben."

"I love you. I can't imagine ever wanting to spend the rest of my life with anyone else, Moriah—but I can't stay. I have to go back."

They looked into one another's eyes, both searching desperately for a way to solve the problem. Both miserable as they contemplated the very real possibility that they had no idea how to solve this problem.

"There's a small airport here on Manitoulin," Ben said. "Maybe you could fly out."

"I tried that once."

"And?"

"I threw up and begged the pilot to let me out."

"That kind of thing happens to a lot of people their first time in the air, Moriah, especially in a small plane."

"He hadn't started the motor, Ben. "

"Oh." He scratched his chin. "You were a child, sweetheart. It would be different now."

"It was last month. I thought my chest would explode. It's not the method, Ben. It's the island. I'm hard-wired to think it's the only place I can be safe."

"What about some kind of therapy?"

"There are no psychologists or psychiatrist here. Even if there were, I saw a show on TV about panic disorder or whatever it is that I have. Even with professional help, it takes years to overcome."

"Years?"

"That's what the TV psychiatrist said."

He groaned. "We don't have years, Moriah."

"I know, but at least, you don't have to go back yet. We still have time to try to figure something out."

"No we don't." He glanced up at her, misery written on his face. "I have to go back tomorrow."

Chapter Thirty-Six

"Why?" She couldn't keep a note of hysteria from creeping into her voice. "Why are you leaving tomorrow?"

It was a bad joke. It had to be

Ben's eyes were serious. It was no joke.

"Abraham called this morning. Violet is sick. He's terrified of losing her, but she's worried about leaving the Yahnowa without someone there who can stabilize things. I speak several tribal dialects. I need to go and try to help."

"Can't the Yahnowa be left alone for a while?"

"Of course, they can. They aren't children. They've been taking care of themselves for centuries, but you don't know Violet. That tribe is her family. She fusses over them like a mother hen. I promised I'd come immediately because I was afraid they would delay their departure until I did."

"But what about the work here?"

"I finished laying the final run of stone on the tower this morning. You can take it from here, Moriah."

She could finish the tower, but she could not lose Ben. Not now. Not ever. She needed his presence in her life like she needed oxygen.

"What if I said you had to make a choice, the Yahnowa or me?"

Ben looked at her a long time before answering. "You'd never do that."

LOVE'S JOURNEY ON MANITOULIN ISLAND: MORIAH'S FORTRESS

"I would, too."

"You're only saying that because you're hurting."

"You already know the language." She knew she sounded desperate, but she couldn't help it. "You could finish it here and find someone else to relieve Abraham and Violet."

"You are right. I could finish the translation here. What you don't understand is that, until I created an alphabet for the Yahnowa, theirs was a language that was a spoken language only. I still have to teach them how to read and write that language. I can't just drop a Bible translation on them and walk away. It would just be a bunch of pages with marks on it. Plus, there is the problem of teaching some of the leaders the other languages they need to know to protect themselves in the future, like Portuguese, which is the language of the Brazilian government. I've already made a lot of progress with some of the young adults, who are eager to learn. My friend, Fusiwe, is already proficient in spoken English and learns fast. Soon, he will become a real leader for the Yahnowa, and as the miners and timber companies encroach, the Yahnowa are going to need men and women who can communicate enough to stand up for themselves. I can't drop the work, Moriah. I just can't."

It was all so much more complicated than she'd imagined. He really was going to have to go back.

"What if I never get any better? What if I can't ever go with you?"

"That won't happen. Someday, you'll leave this island, and you will come to be with me. You are too strong of a person not to overcome this."

"How can you be so sure?"

"Because I know you. I know how determined you are. How strong you are. And I'll pray for you. My prayer will be that we can be together, without you having to remain imprisoned on this island."

"And if God chooses not to answer those prayers? If I can never leave?"

Ben stood and drew her to him. He held her tightly and kissed her. It was not a tentative kiss. It was not a gentle kiss. It was the kiss of a man laying claim to the woman he had chosen.

When they broke apart, she gasped.

"If you can't come to me, I'll come to you," Ben said. "but only after I've fulfilled my promise."

"How long will that take?"

"Too long, Moriah. For my sake, promise me you'll fight."

"I'm already fighting." Her chin trembled. "It's not working."

He glanced at his watch. "It's past midnight. There will be very little traffic. You've been going to the bridge alone. Go now—with me."

Moriah gave him a long, measuring look. "I don't think it will help, but I'll go one more time. With you."

Chapter Thirty-Seven

It took them a half-hour to reach the bridge. Moriah clutched the door handle of the truck and stared straight ahead.

The bridge had one lane. A light at both ends managed the traffic. There were no cars around at the moment. Everyone seemed to be tucked away for the evening. The town had shut down. A pedestrian could walk across the bridge on the walkway and pretty much have the bridge to themselves.

Ben pulled up and let the engine idle.

"What's the best way to do this, Moriah? Do you want me to try driving you across again?"

"No. Making a rush at it intensifies the fear. The farthest I've ever gotten is on foot, slowly, where I know I have some control."

"And I'll go with you?"

"You'd better." Moriah gave him a crooked smile. "You're the one who's making me do this."

Ben parked, turned off the truck, and then helped Moriah down from the cab. She usually hopped out by herself, but tonight was different. She still wore her fancy bridesmaid's clothes. He slammed the door shut and put his hand on her waist as they walked toward her iron nemesis.

"Looks pretty solid to me," he encouraged.

She stopped in front of it. "Funny thing, Ben. That solid-looking bridge has a trick of turning into a fragile, swinging rope bridge the minute I step onto it. I don't think I'll attempt it in heels."

"Want me to carry them for you?"

"Please." She removed her shoes and handed them to him.

"Your bare feet are lovely," he said, gallantly.

She laughed. "My feet are the last things I'm worried about, Ben, but thanks, anyway."

He was pleased to hear her laughter, but he had meant what he said. She had beautiful feet. Right now, in the unaccustomed sheer stockings, they looked especially enhancing. He glanced closer—was that polish?

"You got a pedicure!" he exclaimed as she placed her stocking-clad foot onto the metal.

"It seemed like a good idea at the time." Her breathing had already become ragged, but she slowly stepped out onto the walkway, grasping the iron banister with both hands. "It might help if you held onto me."

He stuffed her shoes into his jacket pockets and grabbed the hand she held back toward him

"You can do this, sweetheart." He squeezed her fingers.

Even though the bridge was solid steel, Moriah scooted her feet like a tightrope walker, holding onto him and the hand rail as though she might, at any moment, fall.

And yet, there was absolutely nothing to cause her to lose her balance. The bridge and walkway was heavy and solid.

She began to pant, as though she had been running a race, even though she had traveled only a few feet. They slowly worked their way further onto the bridge, one inch at a time, when he heard a high keening sound come from her throat.

"I'm here, Moriah honey. I won't let you fall. You're safe." He tightened his grip. She shuffled a few more feet and stopped.

"Look down, Ben." Her eyes were shut. "Look down and tell me what you see."

"Water."

"How far down?"

"You could fish off this bridge, Moriah, or easily jump in and swim to shore if you wanted to."

She nodded. "Hold me for a moment."

He wrapped his arms around her. Her heart beat so hard and fast against his chest that he could feel it through his shirt. He held her to him, willing her heart to slow, to normalize.

Ben felt Moriah's pulse slow ever so slightly. In one part of his brain, he realized that anyone observing them would think they were merely engaged in a lover's embrace. No one could possibly imagine the battle this poor girl was waging. Finally, Moriah unwrapped her arms from around his waist. She turned and stared out at the water below.

"It's only a bridge," she said angrily, "and it's only water! And I'm not five years old anymore!"

"That's right, lass," he said, encouragingly. "It's only a bridge. It's only water, and you are most definitely not a child anymore."

She pulled away from him, placed her hands on her hips and fell into the stance he had seen so often, feet planted far apart, shoulders back, ready to take on yet another project. Through some miracle, the strong, capable Moriah was back.

"Are we going the rest of the way?" he asked.

"Absolutely." She grabbed his hand. "This time, I'm going to do it! I really am, Ben. I can feel it."

Ben's heart soared.

They had almost reached the halfway point of the bridge when a huge semi-truck approached, shifted into a lower gear, and began to cross. Ben felt the beginning vibration of the bridge escalate to a thunderous roar as every bolt and nut in the metal bridge shook in its casing.

The truck was, Ben supposed, driven by a hardworking man, who was merely delivering needed goods to the island, but as the diesel-spewing monster rattled and shook its way onto the bridge, it felt to him like the spawn of Satan.

Moriah froze.

Ben was not a cursing man, but he came close as the heavy truck chewed its way across the bridge, rumbling ominously close to them.

The wind in its wake blew Moriah's hair and dress every which way, and he felt her begin to tremble.

"I want to go back," she whispered.

"Please, sweetheart," he begged. "It was only a truck. You can finish this."

"I want to go back." Her voice was normal, reasonable, as though she were discussing the weather.

"Please try once more, lass," he coaxed.

Her fingers had a death grip on the handrail. Her knuckles had turned white.

"It's only a bridge," he reminded her. "It's only water, remember?"

"Get me off of here."

"Okay. Calm down. I'll help you off."

"NOW!"

Ben didn't hesitate. He picked her up and carried her the few yards back to the earth of Manitoulin Island, Moriah's personal haven—or prison—then propped her against her pickup.

His heart broke as she stood there, gasping for breath, in torn stockings, her pretty dress bedraggled, strands of carefully curled hair sticking to her tear-stained face. She was clenching and unclenching her hands, and her eyes were wild.

"Thank you," she gasped. "Thank you for getting me off there. I couldn't breathe."

"If it hadn't been for the truck, you'd have made it."

"There was a waterfall under the bridge. It made a roaring noise."

"What waterfall?" Ben looked around. "I didn't see a waterfall."

"The one we had to cross to get to the convent, after…"

"After your parents were killed?"

Moriah nodded.

"What happened on that bridge, Moriah?"

"We nearly fell off." Her chest heaved, and her fists spasmodically grabbed handfuls of the skirt of her dress. Her eyes were staring at something far, far away.

"How?"

"Akawe dropped both his spear and our food trying to hang on. The waterfall was so loud, and it kept the footbridge wet and slippery. Akawe had never crossed it with a little girl clutching at him, throwing him off balance. He shouted at me. He said I nearly got us killed."

"I'm so sorry." Ben grabbed her hands, turned them palms up, and kissed them. Then, he kissed her nose and cheeks and forehead, pushing away the tear-mangled hair with his hands.

She responded to his kisses by lifting her face to his warmth and comfort. Her breathing slowed and her eyes focused.

"Don't give up on me, Ben," she said. "Please don't give up on me. I'll fight this. I promise. I want so much to be with you. I'm so sorry. I'm so sorry."

"Don't." His held her and his lips grazed her hair. "It's all right. You don't have to do this ever again. I won't put you through this ever again."

"What do you mean?"

"I have to go back, and I have to finish my work, but I'll be back. If you'll wait for me, I'll come back as soon as I can. I'll get as much work done as possible. I'll ask Nicolas to hunt hard for someone who can replace me, then I'll return."

"To stay?"

"Eventually, to stay."

"How can you do that? You made a promise."

"We'll have to be apart for a while, then I'll come back and never leave you again."

Moriah shook her head. "I can't let you imprison yourself here because of me."

"Most men would consider living on this island with you a paradise, not a prison. I happen to be one of them."

"You will resent me."

"Never."

"I'm not…normal."

"I don't know anyone who is, Moriah."

"You are."

Ben laughed then, a deep, rich laugh that rose from the irony of a childhood spent pulling a father out of bars, scrounging for scraps of food, and stuffing his childhood fears so deep he was amazed he hadn't more phobias than Moriah.

"I'm not even certain what "normal" is, lass. There are only two things I know for certain: I love the Lord, and I love you. You aren't getting rid of me just because you're, let's say—a little bit bridge challenged."

"Okay." Moriah drew a deep breath. "At least, we accomplished one good thing tonight."

"What's that?"

"Tonight, with you beside me, I went the farthest I've ever gone."

Chapter Thirty-Eight

The mist rising from the lake was so dense it nearly hid the sunrise as Ben loaded his few possessions into the back of Moriah's truck.

"I guess that about does it." He swung into the passenger side.

"I guess."

He rolled down the window and hung his elbow out. "Do we have time to drive out to the lighthouse before we go? I'd like to see it one more time. With you."

Moriah swallowed past the lump in her throat. "Sure."

As they drove out the road that Jack had built, the limestone tower rose ghost-like before them, silvery in the mist.

"We did a good job together," she said.

"You'll do a good job without me." He turned toward her and laid his arm along the seat behind her. "Don't let the crew slack off just because I'm not here."

"Slack off?" she scoffed. "I'll make them work harder."

Ben tweaked her ponytail. "Right. You're such a slave driver. Keep Jack on the straight and narrow, too. Okay?"

"He had *better* stay on the straight and narrow. Alicia is pregnant again."

"Lucky man."

"You think so?"

"Yes, I think so. I can't think of anything I'd like more than you and a houseful of kids."

Moriah's throat constricted at the thought of being apart from this man for so long. "Will you be able to write to me?"

"Communication in the jungle is difficult. I can't promise much."

Moriah wiped away a renegade tear. She would not cry and make leaving more difficult for him.

"Have you heard from the guy we took the desk to, yet?" Ben said. "It won't be long before you'll be completely finished and can install that."

"No. He's really good and stays pretty backed up. When I took it to him, he said it might take a couple of months to get around to it."

The old desk held little interest to her, right now. It probably held little interest to Ben, as well. He was just trying to make conversation, trying to make this easier for her. Nothing could make this easier for her.

"We have to go if you're going to make it to the Chi-Cheemaun on time," she said. "You'll enjoy riding in it. Most people do."

"It doesn't matter." He caressed the back of her neck. It was a small gesture, but she cherished it.

As they drove to the dock, Ben, for once, wasn't talkative. He seemed preoccupied and distracted, as though he were already winging his way to the Amazon. She wanted to hear his voice, so she nervously asked questions she already knew the answer to.

"Did you get everything?"

"Yes. I didn't have that much to pack."

"Do you have enough money? There's an ATM at the ferry, and I have extra in my account."

"Nicolas paid me before he left."

"Do you need to grab anything at the store? Snacks? Magazines?"

"No."

She gave up and drove.

When they arrived, there was a long line of cars waiting to board.

Moriah could see the ones in front driving over the huge gangplank and being swallowed up by the giant boat. She gave a slight shiver.

"Don't get stuck in that line, Moriah; pull over and I'll walk the rest of the way."

Moriah obediently pulled into the parking lot and climbed out of the truck as Ben lifted out his bags. She reached to help, but he shook his head.

"I've got to carry them on board, anyway."

She watched him shouldering his bags. He seemed so distracted and preoccupied, she wondered if he would even remember to kiss her good-bye.

"Ben?" she said in a small voice. "You will come back, won't you? Someday?"

He didn't answer; he just gazed at the huge ferry. Then, he removed a canvas bag from his shoulder and handed it to her.

"What's this?" she asked.

"Two dozen notebooks with the first twenty-three books of the New Testament translated into Yahnowa. Five years of my life. I planned to find a copier machine before I left, but everything snowballed, and I never did. Will you find one and mail the copies to me? Nicolas can tell you how to send them."

"You're going to trust me with them?"

"You're the only person in the world that I would trust with such a task. They'll probably be safer with you than with me."

"I'll take good care of them. You're right. There needs to be copies." Her voice was solemn, but her heart was a little lighter. She now knew absolutely that he would come back. He had entrusted his life's work to her, and she would protect it with her own.

There were people milling about them now, and she knew there would be no last, passionate embrace.

"I love you." He briefly brushed her lips with his. "Promise me you'll wait for me."

"I'll wait for you the rest of my life."

Ben smiled. "Let's pray it doesn't take that long."

One more kiss and he strode away. His broad shoulders easily carried the heavy bags.

She clutched the bag of notebooks to her chest for comfort.

He turned and called back, "If anything happens to me, give those to Nicolas. He'll know what to do." Then he waved and disappeared into the maw of the ferry.

If something happened to him? What a terrible thought! Nothing could happen to him. He had to come back here to her.

She ran then, to the edge of the island, watching the giant ferry, hungry for one last glimpse of him.

It seemed to take forever, but as the ferry pulled away from the dock, Ben reappeared on deck. Their eyes locked. She waved with one hand, clutching the canvas bag with the other. Ben waved back, then fisted his right hand and brought it to his heart.

Moriah did the same in reply. She knew what the gesture meant. Ben would come back to her, even if it took years. He had promised. And she would wait for him, even if it took years. She had promised. She had faith that, someday, a preacher would hear their vows. Someday, they would sign a marriage certificate and become man and wife. But a lasting covenant was being made, an oath taken, in that silent gesture they held until she could no longer see him because of the distance and the tears.

She grasped the rusted metal of the guardrail and strained to see. Rain began to fall, creating a gauzy curtain between her and the ferry, which now dipped beneath the horizon. The only thing separating her and Ben was wind and rain.

The panic began to set in as he disappeared. What if this was the last time she saw him? What if something bad *did* happen to him?

She could hire a speedboat to take her out to the ferry. She could hire a small plane to take her to the airport in Toronto where he was first headed. She could...she could...

She didn't even own a passport.

The only thing separating her from Ben was her own weakness and fear.

As the people around her ran for shelter, Moriah was in so much emotional pain, she fell to her knees and curled herself over the bag that held Ben's notebooks, shielding them from the rain.

As the rain beat against her body, she pounded the earth with her fist. "I can fix anything, Lord," she sobbed. "You *know* I can fix anything—but I can't fix me. I'm broken, and I can't fix me. I've tried and tried, but I can't fix me!"

Author's Note

I was surprised to discover that during the 1800's and early 1900's, an era when it was taken for granted that a woman should be paid less than a man, over a hundred women kept the lights burning in lighthouses all over the United States and Canada. Most were women who were already familiar with the job, and who were granted the right to continue the work of their deceased husbands and fathers. They were given pay equal to their male counterparts long before women won the right to vote.

Many took on this hazardous job while also raising large families. Most impressive of all were the women who rowed out alone in storms to rescue those who would otherwise have perished.

Sometimes they faced starvation in the north when the ships that tended the lights could not break through the spring ice to bring provisions. They made hundreds of weary trips up staircases to carry fuel and supplies to keep the light burning. They went without sleep night after night to ensure the lights did not go out. They struggled with loneliness, danger, sickness, sleeplessness, and isolation while keeping those beacons of hope and guidance shining out upon the turbulent waters.

It is impossible to calculate the vast numbers of lives and ships they saved.

Modern day people love the romantic notions of lighthouses. The endurance and dedication of the old light keepers grabs the heart and excites the imagination. Many history buffs devote much of their lives to researching and preserving the lore and history of our remaining lighthouses.

As I researched this series of books, that fact created a problem for me as an author. I try to record the settings of my books as accurately as possible. In this case, it was my beloved Manitoulin Island that I wanted to describe. I did not think choosing an existing lighthouse as a backdrop for a fictional family was going to be well-received by those who have meticulously researched the struggles of the actual families who lived in specific lighthouses.

So, I made one up.

I chose the general location of Providence Bay (which I rename Tempest Bay) where a lighthouse once stood before it burned down. I took great license with the immediate area, creating a peninsula and nearby fishing resort that does not exist. The characters I put in the lighthouse were not based on anyone I know. Michael's Bay (which I rename Gabriel's Bay) is Manitoulin's only ghost town.

Lighthouses similar to the one I describe do exist, however. I chose to pattern Moriah's lighthouse after the Imperial Towers built around the Great Lakes in the early 1800's. They had the stonework that I needed for the story. I read extensively and visited Great Lakes lighthouses to be as accurate as possible in my descriptions. I apologize to lighthouse historians for any mistakes I might have made.

The Yahnowa tribe where Ben lives and works does not exist. However, I tried to make the customs, habits, and habitats as believable and accurate as possible based on my research into some of the larger Amazonian rainforest tribes. A warning, though. Studying the treatment of the indigenous tribes of the Amazon is heartbreaking.

The phobia with which Moriah struggles, does exist. My hope is that as we watch her battle against fear unfold, it might help us face our own demons with a bit more courage.

-Serena

My Heartfelt Thanks To:

. . . .

Charlie Robertson, owner of the once-famous rock shop on Manitoulin Island. I appreciate the example you have been of choosing joy in spite of great loss.

Mamie (Coriell) Robertson, my transplanted cousin, who followed her heart to Manitoulin Island to be with Charlie. Thank you for telling us about the island so many years ago.

Wanda Whittington, Charlie's granddaughter. Thank you for patiently sharing your knowledge of your beloved Manitoulin Island with me and for your amazing hospitality.

My family, for taking the time to help me explore and research the island. The depth of your continued support and encouragement continues to astonish and humble me.

My church who so lovingly took care of me and my family during my husband's final illness.

About the Author

Best Selling author, Serena B. Miller, has won numerous awards, including the RITA and the CAROL. A movie, Love Finds You in Sugarcreek, was based on the first of her Love's Journey in Sugarcreek series, and won the coveted Templeton Epiphany award. Another movie based on her novel, An Uncommon Grace, recently aired on the Hallmark channel. She lives in southern Ohio in a house that her husband and three sons built. It has a wraparound porch where she writes most of her books. Her mixed-breed rescue dog, Bonnie, keeps her company while chasing deer out of the yard whenever the mood strikes. Her Manitoulin Island series is a labor of love based on many visits to the beautiful island.

www.serenabmiller.com

More books by Serena B. Miller

LOVE'S JOURNEY ON MANITOULIN ISLAND SERIES:

Love's Journey on Manitoulin Island: Moriah's Lighthouse - Book I
Love's Journey on Manitoulin Island: Moriah's Fortress - Book II
Love's Journey on Manitoulin Island: Moriah's Stronghold - Book III

LOVE'S JOURNEY IN SUGARCREEK SERIES:

Love's Journey in Sugarcreek: The Sugar Haus Inn - Book I
(Formerly : Love Finds You in Sugarcreek, Ohio)
Love's Journey in Sugarcreek: Rachel's Rescue - Book II
Love's Journey in Sugarcreek: Love Rekindled - Book III

THE UNCOMMON GRACE SERIES (AMISH):

An Uncommon Grace - Book I
Hidden Mercies - Book II
Fearless Hope - Book III

MICHIGAN NORTHWOODS SERIES (HISTORICAL):

The Measure of Katie Calloway - Book I
Under a Blackberry Moon - Book II
A Promise to Love - Book III

SUSPENSE:

A Way of Escape

COZY MYSTERY:

The Accidental Adventures of Doreen Sizemore

NON-FICTION:

More Than Happy: The Wisdom of Amish Parenting

VISIT SERENABMILLER.COM TO SIGN UP FOR
SERENA'S NEWSLETTER AND TO CONNECT WITH SERENA.

CPSIA information can be obtained
at www.ICGtesting.com
Printed in the USA
LVOW08s0145050917
547553LV00001B/136/P